The Changeling Quest

Children of the Fae

The Changeling Quest

Children of the Fae

Maria Moloney

OUR STREET BOOKS

Winchester, UK
Washington, USA

First published by Our Street Books, 2013
Our Street Books is an imprint of John Hunt Publishing Ltd., Laurel House, Station Approach, Alresford, Hants, SO24 9JH, UK
office1@jhpbooks.net
www.johnhuntpublishing.com
www.ourstreet-books.com

For distributor details and how to order please visit the 'Ordering' section on our website.

Text copyright: Maria Moloney 2012

ISBN: 978 1 78099 405 5

A CIP catalogue record for this book is available from the British Library.

Design: Stuart Davies

Cover: Eoghan Walsh

Printed and bound by CPI Group (UK) Ltd, Croydon, CR0 4YY

We operate a distinctive and ethical publishing philosophy in all areas of our business, from our global network of authors to production and worldwide distribution.

For my granddaughters, Holly Majella Susan, Elizabeth (Libby) Marie, Tyler-Jean Lily, Isla Rose, and the newest arrival, Lilia Robyn.

Prologue

Zalen was running out of time. He had to get to Vrogoly by midnight and had no choice but to travel by ley tunnel. Wiser fae folk took the longer routes, but no, not him. Even though the thought of the leys terrified him, he would rather risk his life than face the fury of his mistress. And as the Vrogoly Gateway was the only way into the human world this night, foolish as it was, he had no choice in the matter, so the leys it had to be.

All his life, until now, he had managed to avoid travelling the ley tunnels. They had killed his brother, so he knew how dangerous they were. He could of course dump the baby and flee the realm. But if he did, his mistress would surely come after him and he would be forced to travel the leys…several of them. That, or escape into the human world, and these days nowhere was safe in the human world.

The Five Rivers Gateway opened for one hour before and after midnight each night. Once there, he would step into the portal and the energy of the ley would whisk him downwards and carry him along the underground passageway to the Vrogoly Gateway. In such a way, folk could travel from gateway to gateway and get to different parts of the realm much faster than by normal means. That was where the danger lay. The tunnels, dark and narrow as a coffin, had jagged rocks and spiky tree roots protruding from the walls. Sometimes they constricted to the width of a snake's path. When Zalen had found his brother's bruised and battered body lying outside a gateway all those years ago, his bones broken and crushed, he had vowed never to travel the leys.

Zalen shuddered and shutting out the horrible visions this thought conjured up, he concentrated on the way ahead and scurried on along the narrow path. Around him stretched miles of wild purple hills and woods of grand oak. The grass moved in ripples, although no wind blew, and the trees began to sway upon his arrival as though the land itself could sense his presence. As long as no one else did, he thought, it was imperative no one saw the baby he carried. At least that had been the order from his mistress. Luckily, so far, he had not seen a soul.

Five minutes later, he left the path and cut across a field, the full moon lighting his way. The path, hardly trodden, hampered his progress. Still, it took a few precious minutes off his journey time, would avoid the village, and bring him much closer to the Five Rivers Gateway.

He skirted a row of trees feeling secure that at least few knew the route and he was unlikely to be spotted. If anyone was so much as to catch a glimpse of him, he must dump the realm baby in the nearest dry ditch, leave her there, and go back for her later. But it would cost valuable time and he had none.

The moon disappeared behind a cloud just as Zalen scrambled over the stile and stepped back onto the path. He found himself plunged into darkness so abruptly, he promptly tripped over a large stone, only just managing to save himself from falling. Jolted, the realm baby stirred in his arms. The moon reappeared and Zalen glanced down. His heart skipped a beat. The baby slept; the herbs his mistress had given her were doing their job.

For a moment, he stood transfixed and found it hard to look away. It was almost as if something compelled him to gaze down at the child – at the way her ebony locks framed her heart-shaped face, her long thick lashes rested on her creamy cheeks and her mouth pursed into a tiny rosebud.

His insides squirmed, she would survive travelling the ley, but as soon as they reached the human world, he would have to kill her. A simple task his mistress has said, but then she did not have to do it. The gold bracelet the baby wore protected her, but once she passed through the gateway, it would lose its power and he could remove it from her wrist and take it back to his mistress.

The realm baby smiled in her sleep and Zalen cast his eyes up to Lady Moon and made a wish. He shook his head vigorously to refocus his attention and hastened onwards.

It was close to midnight when Zalen reached Five Rivers; his arms ached from the weight of the baby, which was so much bigger and heavier than a spriggan child, not that he had held that many spriggan babies...horrible little things even if they were of his own kind. He had crossed two bridges and so far, all was well.

Now standing on the third bridge, he looked furtively around checking no one else was planning to use the gateway this night. The rushing water beneath him drowned out all other sounds as it hastened to meet the other four rivers, a few feet away. No one would hear his approach. He looked ahead of him, not a soul in sight, satisfied he stepped off the bridge. Two more minutes would bring him to the grove of trees he was seeking.

The oak, ash and hawthorn trees stood close together under a star strewn sky, moonbeams appearing to highlight them. To the eye, the trees seemed perfectly normal, but there was something magnetic about them as they beckoned all towards them. Zalen paused on the edge of the triangle of trees. Some folk were more susceptible than others, to the power that lay within. Perhaps he was like his brother. Zalen shivered and shook the thought from his mind. Getting into this mess was his biggest regret, but now he had, there was no going back.

Not wanting to think about it a second longer, bracing himself, Zalen stepped into the gateway. A flash of blue light momentarily blinded him and before he had time to blink, a force whipped him off his feet and into the whorl spinning him around and around on the spot. An enormous pressure knocked his breath out of him as the ley sucked him downwards and yanked him along the tunnel feet first.

The energy dragged him into more and more whorls, banging him into tree roots and rocks as he went. Several times the pull of the ley almost tore the realm baby from his arms, it was already a strain to keep himself as still as possible, he was tempted to just let her go and suffer the wrath of his mistress. Somehow, his resolve crept back in and he hung onto her as the ley energy carried him onwards, battering him about like a twig in a storm.

Two minutes later, he already wished himself dead, anything to stop the torment, until the thought struck him he might well be before he reached his destination.

When he at last arrived at the Vrogoly Gateway, indicated by a dazzling blue circle of light, a magical energy whipped him upwards feet first, into the world of humans. He landed with a thump on the grass next to the burial mound, winded, and quivering like an aspen leaf. The realm baby rolled from his arms onto the grass and he left her where she lay.

He decided it would be wise to stay put for a few minutes to try to control the shaking. He patted his arms, squeezed his legs and wiggled his toes, relieved to find he had no broken bones. Plenty of bruises and scratches, but yes, it could have been much worse.

A whimper alerted him, the journey must have lessened the effects of the sleeping herbs and soon the baby would be fully awake. Not being able to delay any longer, he scooped her up, dragged himself to his feet, staggered to the field gate and scrambled over into the garden.

The silver moonlight snaked along the winding cobbled path. Ahead of him, the crooked house loomed out of the darkness just as his mistress had described it, centuries old and barely able to hold itself up. Everything sagged. Black timbers made a criss-cross pattern over the ochre walls, while some of the gabled windows tilted so much, it seemed as if the house could collapse at any time. The walls buckled under the weight of the roof, causing the windows to lie out of alignment.

He scanned the facade. The top windows were situated high

off the ground. Pinpointing the third window from the right, he decided he would have no problems clambering up as long as he could use both hands.

Making a sling of the blanket, he tied it around his neck so the baby lay close to him. He looked down into indigo eyes, and in turn, they looked back at him, boring into his very soul. She began to whimper, again his insides took a tumble and he tore his eyes away. Hurriedly, he scaled the wall of the house getting a good grip by digging his long nails into the crisscrossing black timbers.

At last reaching the window, Zalen concentrated hard on loosening the catch. His magic was not strong, so it was no easy task, but coupled with a bit of brute force he pulled open the window and jumped over the sill in a trice.

Standing in the room it took a few moments for his eyes to adjust to the darkness. A bed stood against the wall and he could see a small child lying in it, but this was not the one he sought, for she was too old.

Looking further, he spied the crib in the corner and scuttled over. Sure enough, the human baby lay in it fast asleep. He quickly switched the babies, tying the human baby around his neck in the makeshift sling.

In the crib, the realm baby began to cry. He searched for a cushion and found one on a miniature chair. Taking it, he approached the crib and held it above her face. Her bottom lip quivered and Zalen hesitated. He could not do it, could not kill this little thing.

Behind him, a fierce wind suddenly blew in through the open window almost knocking him off his feet. The window shot outwards and began to bang against the wall. A screeching black shadow flew through it, circled the room, and hovered above him for a second before diving down at him.

Zalen tried to use the cushion as a shield to protect his face from the terrible onslaught as the black fiend stabbed at his head and hands with its sharp hooked beak. The realm baby was now screaming like a banshee and the human baby joined in. The blood from the wounds trickled into Zalen's eyes, blinding him. Dropping the cushion, he brushed the blood away with his sleeve and ran to the window.

He was climbing out when he glimpsed a human male standing in the doorway on the other side of the room. Dropping over the sill, he tumbled down the wall and jumped into the garden. He landed awkwardly, grabbed his foot and cursed.

Trying to ignore the pain, he struggled to his feet and seeing a movement above, he looked back up at the window. The human male stood there looking down at him, a look of horror and astonishment on his face.

Zalen immediately recognised the mess he had left behind, he had been seen and the realm baby still lived, his mistress would have his head for this. Now all he could do was to cut his losses and at least get the human baby back through the gateway. There was one consolation, the realm baby could not stay in the human world more than one day longer than her eleventh birthday without visiting the realms or she would die anyway, a failsafe curse put on her by his mistress, he would remind her of it and hope it would satisfy her.

Zalen ran for his life along the pathway. Hearing the beat of wings above him, he attempted to protect his face with his arms, but the fiend continually dived at him, its great claws trying to gouge out his eyes.

A shout came from behind – the human male was hurtling up the path after him – what a nightmare this had turned out to be.

It was only when he reached the mound and the blue flash of light carried him back through the gateway that tendrils of fear and dread stole up his spine, the hairs prickled the back of his neck as his throat closed up threatening to choke him. Not only had he failed to kill the realm baby, he had forgotten to take the bracelet.

Chapter One

On the outside, it looked just like any other burial mound or tumulus, of which there were hundreds in the area. A dome shaped mound or hill, covered with grass with a shallow ditch all around. The difference between this one and others in the immediate area was it was larger than most, and sat in the field – their field – right at the bottom of their garden, on the edge of Salisbury Plain.

Tara could just see the hare sitting beneath it. She eyed it suspiciously, wondering whether to go out or stay indoors in the dry warmth of the kitchen, and get on with icing Niamh's birthday cake.

It was funny now looking back, how scared she used to be of the mound. Every Halloween a mist encircled it and strange lights would appear and disappear. She would sneak to the window and have a quick peek to see if any ghosts lurked there, but seeing the darting lights, would run and hide behind the couch trembling. But she was younger then.

All day the rain had poured down, and the large brown hare had sat by the mound just as her sister Niamh had said it would. Surely, it wasn't natural a hare would sit there day after day for a whole week. Tara was suspicious it had something to do with the gateway. And there was a gateway in the mound, Niamh was sure of it, a magical gateway that led to the Otherworld. Perhaps something had changed. Something that might give a clue to whether the gateway was really there and convince her Niamh was right.

Tara moved from the window seat, pushed her feet into her shoes, which sat by the back door, and went outside to investigate. She hurried up the garden path, her feet slipping and sliding on the wet leaves shed by the gnarled apples trees, which still held a few misshapen apples. Fat raindrops fell down from a slate grey cloud overhead. Pleased to see the sky clearing from the west, she hoped by midnight, it would be dry. It was one thing sneaking out in the dark with a full moon lighting the way, but if it turned out to be wet and gloomy, it would surely be a miserable experience.

She reached the padlocked gate, the metal of it wet and cold, still she climbed over into the small field anyway.

The mound sat at the opposite side, like a stark and luscious emerald. A group of hawthorn trees obscured her from the hare so she ran up keeping herself concealed behind them.

The smell of wet grass tickled her nostrils and she sneezed. Laughing softly to herself, she peeked around the trees expecting the hare to have run away in fright, but it hadn't moved. It sat there, stock still, its mustard eyes staring at her. Tara found it hard to look away. It was as if the hare could see right inside her and even read her thoughts.

Telling herself she was being silly, she stepped out from the trees and tried to frighten it by waving her arms about, but still it sat there.

'Shoo...go on, get lost!' she encouraged.

It didn't flinch.

Maybe it isn't real, she thought. Scanning the ground, she picked up a stone and threw it. The stone landed right at the hare's feet and Tara had an instant of misgiving as its eyes flashed ominously. The hare sprang up, startling her. She stumbled sideways as it leapt towards her and she fell onto the cold wet grass.

The hare was almost on her, when hearing a shriek, she looked up to see a flash of black and a huge raven swooped down so close, she could see the blue sheen on its gargantuan wings.

The hare stopped in mid-flight, and crouched close to the ground. Its malevolent eyes glared at her, and leaping up on its hind legs, it turned in the air and ran zigzag across the Plain.

The raven flew up, the whoosh of its wings causing her to fall flat on her back, the backdraught from them making her blink. Stunned she could only gawp as it circled the mound and flew off in the same direction as the hare.

A large drop of rain landed on her nose and Tara sat up. 'For heaven's sake!' she said aloud.

Feeling shaken and foolish, she picked herself up from the grass and wiped her hands on the back of her sodden jeans. It might have been weird, but it was only a hare. Just the same, she glanced behind her to check it had gone. An icy prickle ran along her arms as she caught sight of the mound, which suddenly appeared gloomy and threatening. It's just the angle of it, she reasoned, but deep inside she remained unconvinced.

She quickly climbed over the gate and into the garden. Pulling her sleeves down over her hands, she tramped back along the winding path.

The back of the old Tudor house was all higgledy-piggledy and as Tara approached it, she took in every detail. It had been the family home for centuries. She loved the way it looked, as if it had given out a huge sigh, relaxed and drooped. Although it gave the impression it wasn't safe to live in and as if it could fall down at any minute, she hoped it would be around for many more centuries. She was proud of living there. Her friends thought it resembled a large gingerbread house straight from a fairytale. To Tara it was home and she loved it.

She arrived at the back door at the same time as Uncle Fergus, sensibly dressed in bright yellow waterproofs. Opening the door with a flourish, he bowed to her in an exaggerated way, his other hand outstretched. Tara laughed and jumped over the step into the kitchen.

Niamh and Mum were busy there. Niamh took a jug of orange juice from the fridge and poured herself and Mum a glass. As soon as she turned and saw Tara and Uncle Fergus, she put the jug on the big wooden table and fetched more glasses. Meantime, Mum was concentrating on digging out the centre of a pumpkin ready to make a Jack-o'-Lantern. Niamh was lucky her birthday fell on Halloween, as it meant she always had a party.

Tara was relieved to find everything comfortably ordinary and no one suspected anything. She kicked off her shoes and went to the sink to wash the mud off her hands. Changing into dry clothes could wait for a few minutes. She would need to get ready for the party anyway.

'Hello girls, everyone is very busy I see,' said Uncle Fergus. Tara was relieved he didn't question where she'd been.

'Hi,' answered Mum and Niamh in unison.

Tara's hands shook slightly as she fetched the birthday cake from the cooling tray and joined Mum at the kitchen table. It wasn't easy trying to act normal, not that Mum would notice, she always drifted into a world of her own. She never kept still and always managed to find something to do; she never listened to them either, often answering their questions automatically. Uncle Fergus said anxiety caused it and Mum had suffered from it for years.

Tara felt the need to busy herself too and set about making the icing. Pangs of guilt collided with excitement about their plans for later that night.

Uncle Fergus was always cheerful and Tara was glad of it at times. She watched him as he picked up a glass of orange juice and drained it in one go, before pouring another. 'Now my girls, guess where I've been working this morning?' he said, but didn't wait for an answer. '...Just down the road near Stonehenge. It proved to be very interesting.'

'I bet it *proved* to be very cold,' said Tara, imitating his voice. She laughed. Uncle Fergus was an archaeologist and never seemed to notice the cold or damp. Tara and Niamh had been on a couple of digs with him and found it hard and dirty work.

'It was a tad wet, to be sure,' he agreed laughing, shaking the raindrops from his coat. 'It's a privilege though, a real privilege to work there. You'd be surprised what I see on some of my digs.' He took off his boots, leaving muddy patches on the slate floor. 'And what have you two girls been doing with yourselves this morning?'

'Nothing much,' said Niamh. 'Just getting ready for the party and—'

'It's been raining all morning,' Tara quickly interrupted, 'so nothing much really.'

Mum suddenly woke up. 'Speak for yourself. Treacle toffee is made, birthday cake is made, cup cakes made, quiche made, truffles made, brownies made, and jelly is made—'

'Jelly!' Gosh, how old did Mum think they were? Party food covered the table, far too much for herself, Niamh and Lucy. They would be eating jelly sandwiches for days.

'So what sort of tricks have you planned for tonight?' asked Uncle Fergus, glancing up at Niamh. He took off his waterproofs and wiped his face with his mucky fingers, spreading the dirt into the lines around his eyes. He looked comical with his silver streaked hair and beard sticking out all over the place like a scarecrow. But that was Uncle Fergus. He always looked like that, scruffy and rumpled. He had better things to do than worry about his appearance he always said.

'Just the usual things,' said Niamh, and gave Tara a knowing smile. 'We thought we might watch a film later, Mum's made some popcorn. We could play a board game too, now there are four of us.'

'Four of us? What are you on about, Niamh?' asked Tara. 'You mean *three* of us.'

'No four. Lucy...and Jared too.'

'Jared!' Tara was horrified. 'Why would Jared want to come to your silly little birthday party?'

Niamh pulled a face and glowered at her. 'Well, he does. Lucy's not allowed anywhere overnight without him after that time she wandered off and got lost.' She paused and said meaningfully, 'And anyway I want her to sleep over.'

'She must have been five years old when she wandered off. It's pathetic she can't go anywhere without big brother watching her every move. She's not a baby, she's eleven years old!'

'Now, now, girls. I'm sure there's plenty of space for all friends to stay if they want to,' admonished Uncle Fergus.

Abandoning the cake, Tara marched out of the kitchen in disgust. How could Niamh invite Jared behind her back? How embarrassing. They used to be friends, but since they started secondary school, they never mixed at all. Niamh must have done it deliberately. She knew how he irritated her. She and Lucy must be up to something, maybe even trying to push her out as usual. They'd better not be thinking of sneaking off without her.

Niamh came hurrying after her. 'Jared *has* to come,' she said simply. 'Lucy's already told him about the plan, and she won't be able to sleep over unless he's with her.'

'Told him about the plan! You are joking. He must have laughed his socks off!'

'Well, he didn't. Anyway, he'll be company for you. And he *is* your friend.'

'*Used* to be my friend, as you well know. There's no way he'll want to join in our plans. He'll think we made it all up.' Tara was beginning to think she was right and something more was going on. 'So is this your plan? Hoping I won't go?'

'Oh, for goodness sake, stop nagging, Tara. And if you don't keep your voice down none of us will be going anywhere. Jared wants to come, so there. Anyway it'll be more fun with the four of us.'

'This isn't a game, Niamh!' Niamh stared at her intensely, her brows knitting over her midnight eyes. She knew it wasn't a game and Tara shouldn't have said it. She sighed. 'Well, he's with you, not me. Remember that.'

Tara turned and stomped up the narrow wooden staircase. This was all she needed. It was just supposed to be the two of them going to find the gateway. Then Niamh had opened her big mouth to Lucy, and now Jared too. She didn't know why Niamh didn't just go ahead and invite her whole class. Tara groaned, why did she care so much? It might all be a lot of old nonsense and a waste of time. But if that were true, why since that day in the summer holidays had she been unable to think of anything else?

Reaching the bathroom, she decided to take a bath. She needed cooling off time. As she ran the water, she considered why she always let her temper get the better of her. But she knew the answer, nothing was right at home. Mum was getting worse she was sure, and now this business with Niamh and the photos. It was all so unsettling. Someone needed to put things right, and that would have to be herself and she would start this very night.

Tara stepped into the bath and slipped under the water, planning to stay there as long as she could. It calmed her, especially when Niamh annoyed her or Mum wasn't listening. Sometimes, she wished she had an older sister to talk to...or a dad. She was sure she would have got on well with her dad, just as she did with Uncle Fergus. It wasn't that Uncle Fergus didn't talk to her. It was just that he was seldom serious – was always joking around.

Jared was once great fun, until secondary school, when he made new friends; a crowd Tara didn't particularly like – always messing around and hanging out in the village park. She'd befriended a couple of girls from her old school, but nothing was the same anymore, and they lived in town and she didn't get there very often. She lay thinking about when she, Niamh, Jared and Lucy, all used to play together. She sighed. It was no use wishing for those days again.

A bewildering thought caused Tara's eyes to shoot open. She'd been under the water for a while – a long while. Did she fall asleep? The bubble-topped water appeared to be floating above her and she was breathing normally. She abruptly sat up and the water crashed down splashing all over the floor. Now she *was* imagining things. No one could breathe underwater! What was happening to her? She must have had a waking dream. When she thought about it, she hadn't felt right all day, she hoped she wasn't sickening for something.

Tara loved the water. Uncle Fergus called her his water baby. She always thought this was because of her strangely webbed toes. And she had to admit, there was nothing she liked better than to go swimming anywhere, anytime. She swam for the school and for the county. Nowhere did she feel more comfortable than in the water. Not this time though, this was creepy.

She pulled out the plug and while the water drained, quickly rinsed her hair. Tara had a feeling, deep inside her, penetrating her very bones, something was about to happen, and it scared her.

Back in the bedroom, she opened the wardrobe and immediately chose her best dress to wear. Glittering silver, it showed off her long legs. She found a sparkly necklace and a pair of wedge shoes to go with it. Later she could change back into jeans and her trainers before they set off to find the gateway.

After drying her waist length, pale strawberry hair, she twisted it up at the back, fixing it with a large silver clip. She looked in the mirror feeling reasonably satisfied. It would have to do, but secretly she was pleased with the result. She couldn't let Jared think she was as daft as Niamh and Lucy. She was much more sophisticated. Guilt pangs stabbed at her heart, how could she be so angry with Niamh? Tonight she would find out for certain if she was her real sister and if not...

Leaving the room, she avoided the stairs leading down and instead carried on up the second staircase to the attic. Stepping over the obstacle course of musty boxes and books, which wasn't easy in her high shoes, she reached the old wardrobe in the corner and with some effort pulled open the door. Rummaging around, she found the photo album among several others, this one marked by the cheerful sunflowers decorating the cover. A battered wicker chair stood in the corner so she sat down and opened the album.

She stared at the photos under the plastic. Slipping one from its pocket, she compared it to one that lay loose. In one photo, Mum and Dad stood there holding a laughing, chubby baby girl, of about one year old. She had wispy strawberry-blonde hair and pale, lime green eyes, just like her own. Next to Mum, clinging to her skirts, Tara herself stood, aged about three.

In the other photo, it was Mum holding Tara's hand and Uncle Fergus held a baby in his arms. Clearly this was Niamh, recognisable by her mop of curly black hair, pointy ears, dark eyes and skinny limbs. The babies in the two photos looked to be about the same age, but were very different, and there the problem lay.

It had been another rainy day, the worst summer ever, when she and Niamh had first found the album. Mum was having one of her bad days and had been spring-cleaning the house since early morning. Uncle Fergus was in his study and she and Niamh had been helping him sift through some artefacts. When they became bored, he had suggested they go and *mooch* around in the attic. With no better ideas, they had trudged up the stairs. Once in the attic, Tara went over to one corner to look through the old toys, while Niamh wandered around the room picking up odd things, then discarding them.

'Hey, Tara, come and see this,' Niamh had called from across the room. And before Tara had looked up from the pile of old board games she had been rooting through, Niamh had sat down on a box and opened a book. Curious, Tara went over and found it wasn't a book at all, but a photograph album.

Leafing through the album, they saw lots of pictures of a baby girl neither of them had seen before and she lay in the arms of their parents. Ten years had passed since their dad had gone missing. Niamh had been only one year old and Tara three. Tara had no memory of him. Like their great Uncle Fergus, he was an archaeologist and he had gone on an expedition to South America, but had sadly never returned. Uncle Fergus told them it had caused Mum's nervousness and that's why she kept herself busy.

At first, they thought the strange baby must be a cousin or something, but as they turned the pages and saw more photos of their mother, father, the strange baby and a little girl who was quite clearly Tara, it became more and more puzzling.

'That's not me,' said Niamh, her eyebrows knitting together. 'So where am I?'

The pictures of the baby were not the same as the ones of Niamh that lay in the albums downstairs. Tara and Niamh had both queried more than once why there weren't many photos of Niamh when she was a tiny baby, and had been told they were lost. This must be them, only the baby wasn't Niamh unless she had changed overnight.

The photos of Niamh downstairs began at the age of around one year old. A horrible gnawing began in Tara's stomach. Niamh was adopted. But what had happened to the other baby?

Niamh saw it for herself, and neither of them spoke while they took it all in. Tara didn't want to believe it, but it explained a few things, such as why they looked so unalike.

'She must have died or something, how awful,' said Tara at last, her heart heavy.

'No, I don't think so. I think something else happened. Do you remember the story Uncle Fergus used to tell us about the babies and the burial mound?'

Tara thought back, yes, Niamh must mean the story about a mysterious and childlike figure that climbed through a window and swapped two babies. When they were younger, Uncle Fergus had often told them the story and they loved it because it featured two little girls and a house just like theirs, which had a burial mound in the field. In fact, Uncle Fergus had brought it up during a discussion on the history of the mound only yesterday.

'Yes, of course,' said Tara, wondering what Niamh's point was. 'Late on Halloween night, lots of noise and screeching woke the children's parents, and the father rushed along to their room just in time to see a small ugly figure climbing out of the window and a large black bird flying out after it. By the time the mother got there, the baby was screaming in her cot and their other little girl sobbed too. At first in the pandemonium, both parents stood frozen, too stunned to move. The father shook himself out of it and explained what he'd seen. He picked up the older daughter and the mother ran to the cot, and that's when she noticed a strange baby lying there and their own baby had disappeared.'

'And the father...the father,' continued Niamh, she put her finger on her chin and pursed her lips as she recalled the story, 'Well he put down the little girl, went to the window and must have seen something...or someone, as he dashed downstairs, out of the back door. The mother followed and watched everything from the path. By the light of the moon, she saw a small grotesque figure carrying a bundle and the father was chasing it. A flash of blue light illuminated the garden and the mysterious figure, the bundle – this was the baby of course – and the father vanished into it. They had gone through a magical gateway in the mound, into the Otherworld, a place of dragons and fae folk and were never seen again— '

'And in time, the mother thought she'd imagined the whole thing and the little changeling baby gradually became one of the family,' Tara finished, the story whirling around in her head as she tried to figure it all out. 'It was a strange story...and yes it *was* about two babies who were changed over by the fae folk.'

'Tara, don't you get it yet? The baby...the strange baby in the cot...it's *me*.'

Tara stood staring at her little sister. Niamh stared back at her in earnest. She raised one eyebrow, which she always did when she was trying to get you to understand her. Tara shook her head in disbelief. It made sense. It made horrible sense. It was *their* dad who had disappeared through the magical gateway, not on an expedition at all.

Niamh's eyes were bright, too bright. Tara covered Niamh's hands with her own. She was happy the baby wasn't dead, but if Niamh wasn't her sister, she didn't like it one little bit either. But who was she? Where did she come from?

'Wow,' breathed Niamh as the reality sank in further. She frowned and her voice rose to a higher pitch. 'Mum isn't my real mum. And we…*you*…have another sister who was kidnapped.'

'It's just a story, Niamh,' said Tara, giving her a hug. 'Anyway, I don't want you not to be my sister.'

'So why are there two different babies in the photos?'

Niamh jumped up, ran downstairs, and fetched one of the photos of herself with Mum and Uncle Fergus. They compared it to the ones in the album. All it did was confirm their suspicions. They sat side by side, scrutinising them for quite some time. Downstairs, in the albums, they knew there wasn't one photo of Niamh with their father where they could actually see her clearly.

Another thought came to Tara, once, years ago, Jared had said to her their dad hadn't gone missing on an expedition, but had ran off and left them all. She thought he was just being spiteful, until she did some research on the school computer and could find nothing about anyone going missing on such an expedition. In fact, there was no mention of a Cathal McNamara, archaeologist. Maybe Jared had heard something they didn't know, rumours perhaps. If Niamh was right, Tara did have another sister – a sister who was kidnapped and taken through a magical gateway.

Tara and Niamh decided not to mention the album, hiding it in the back of the wardrobe, while they investigated further. They recalled Uncle Fergus had once told them mounds were gateways to the Otherworld. He also told them about an old superstition. It warned about avoiding mounds at certain times of the year.

Later they had asked Uncle Fergus about the story, but he had just laughed and said it was just that…a story, then he winked. Tara also asked for more details about the expedition their dad had gone on, and Uncle Fergus said he would have to tell her later as he was busy with a project and didn't have time, but later never came. This had fuelled their belief the story was true.

They had scrutinised the burial mound more than once, but had never found a gateway. In the story though, it had been on the night of Halloween that the fae folk had changed the babies. Then there were the spooky lights, which appeared every year. So they had formed the plan of sneaking out in the night to see if there really was a gateway. It was the only way to find out if the story held any truth. They might even go through it if it were possible – an exciting adventure just for her and Niamh, until Niamh had opened her big mouth to Lucy that was, now the two of them always seemed to be whispering and making their own plans.

Over the following weeks, Tara had begun to think more and more about the missing baby – her sister. She tried to imagine what she was like now. Was she tall like Tara? Was Dad with her? She hoped he was, because she didn't like the thought of a baby whisked from her home and left alone in some strange place. As much as she wanted a dad, it made her feel so much better to know he might well be looking after her missing sister. Another sister would be great. It wasn't that she didn't love Niamh; it was just that they hardly ever did anything together. Niamh liked to be outdoors whenever she could, with Lucy her best friend. Tara spent a lot of time alone in their room reading.

Tara put the album back in the wardrobe, the excitement once more welling up inside her. Her whole life could change, a dad, a new sister, and she was sure her mum would be much happier too.

She was halfway down the stairs when there was a knock on the front door. Footsteps clattered over the tiled hallway and the click of a latch was followed by Lucy's shrill voice...then a deeper voice...Jared. She didn't feel up to facing him, but decided to get it over with. If he ridiculed them, he could just stay behind. That was all there was to it. Feeling better with her decision, she plodded on down the stairs.

Tara's mum took their coats and hung them up. Niamh was excited and dragged Lucy off into the kitchen, leaving Tara to deal with Jared alone. He grinned at her and winked. As soon as her mum walked back to the kitchen, he leant over and whispered to her, 'Ha and here's me thinking you'd gone all stuffy and boring.'

Tara felt the colour rising to her cheeks, was that what he thought of her. 'Well, better than being an idiot with no brains who can only think of football and uses an entire bottle of gel on his hair every day. Talk about overkill!'

Jared's mouth dropped open with surprise and a hurt expression crept into his eyes. Tara didn't care, spinning around she flounced off after her mum, leaving him standing in the hallway.

Chapter Two

The party wasn't quite over when, with a flourish, Uncle Fergus produced the extra birthday present. He handed Niamh a blue, velvet covered box. Niamh clapped her hands in delight when she saw it, and taking it, slowly opened the lid to reveal a gold bracelet set with a huge stone. Niamh gasped and slipped it straight onto her wrist. When she twisted the bracelet into place, Tara saw the stone was indigo, the exact colour of Niamh's eyes.

'It's gorgeous, Niamh,' gushed Lucy. 'You're so lucky. I wish I had one like that.'

Tara couldn't help feeling a twang of jealousy and wished she had one too.

Niamh gleamed. 'Wow, thanks, Uncle Fergus!' She threw her arms around his neck and gave him a big kiss on the cheek.

'A special gift, for a special girl,' announced Uncle Fergus and for once Tara noticed he looked serious, even concerned.

Mum stared at the bracelet and shook her head as if shaking a thought from her mind. A tear ran down her face, which she brushed away. She laughed nervously. 'Don't mind silly me.'

Tara wondered if Mum ever thought about that night, ten years ago to this very day. The story did say the mum had convinced herself she had imagined things. She hoped Mum did think it was all a dream or something. If the story was actually true, Mum must be really upset on the anniversary of Dad and the real Niamh going missing. And even if it wasn't, Dad had gone missing anyway, so she would still think about that. Today must be hard for her. Tara went over and gave her a hug. Mum smiled at her reassuringly, her eyes saying, *I'm all right – don't worry about me.*

Uncle Fergus went to wash up the dishes, while Mum joined everyone in a rare game of Monopoly. Jared won, which irritated

Tara very much. Why he was so popular at school with the girls she really couldn't fathom. She'd heard mention of his thick brown hair and dreamy grey eyes, while his bigheadedness, arrogance, and tendency to act like a seven-year-old were happily ignored. The fact he was captain of the football team, which had beaten every other school team in the county, just added to his popularity, yet his school reports were awful. Tara would be embarrassed to take home school reports like his, but he just laughed about it and didn't care. Well, she didn't care about him either. He was welcome to all his new friends.

'No one beats me in this,' he bragged.

'Yes they do,' said Lucy, innocently. 'Dad nearly always beats you.'

Jared poked out his tongue.

'Looks like it's all in your imagination,' Tara snapped, finding it hard to keep the sneer from her voice. Jared gave her an intense stare. Well that wiped the smug smile off his face, she thought.

'Well done, Jared,' said Mum, which made Tara feel a bit guilty for being mean. Not that she would let him know. 'How about I fetch the popcorn and you all settle down to watch the film? Then I can go and help Fergus tidy up.'

They all got up from the table and made their way to the living room. Tara pushed in front and reached the living room first so she could sit in the one single chair. No way was she going to end up snuggled up next to Jared on the couch.

Tara thought the film, the latest pirate adventure in a series, would never end. Soon they would be on their own adventure. Restless, she couldn't keep her legs still, and kept wiggling them about. If only it was midnight and they were already safely out of doors. As it was, her main fear was that they would be caught sneaking out, which would not only be the end of all their plans, as they would have to wait until next year before trying again, but they would probably be grounded forever.

As soon as the film finished, she ran over and switched off the TV, the sooner they all went to bed the sooner Mum and Uncle Fergus would.

Niamh caught on. 'I'm sooo tired, we're off to bed aren't we, Lucy?'

'Yes, let's go to bed,' Lucy said in a louder voice than was necessary to carry into the kitchen. Tara closed her eyes and gritted her teeth. The sooner they were all upstairs the better. With a couple of nods of her head, she indicated they should all get going.

'We're off to bed now,' called Tara from the hallway. Mum came out of the kitchen and gave her, Niamh and Lucy a kiss. Uncle Fergus hugged them and ruffled Lucy and Jared's hair.

'I hope you had an exciting day, kids. A birthday to remember, eh, Niamh?'

'It will be—' said Lucy.

'Night,' said Jared. He poked Lucy in the arm.

Tara led the way up the stairs before Lucy had time to put her foot in it again.

It was close to midnight. They had all changed into jeans and jumpers, and now congregated in the bedroom Tara shared with Niamh. Mum and Uncle Fergus had gone to bed early. The time had dragged, and Tara spent much of it trying to keep Niamh and Lucy quiet. Jared was supposed to be sleeping in the guest room, and a few minutes before, Lucy had tapped on his wall and given him the all clear. He now sat on a mattress on the floor with Lucy, clearly thinking the whole thing a hoot.

Tara studied each of them in turn. It was hard to tell what Jared really thought about it all, clearly in a good mood he kept grinning. Lucy looked young for her age, a mini version of Jared, though her brown hair was cut into a bob. Jared had better watch out for her, thought Tara, because she didn't intend to spend the whole adventure babysitting. In comparison, Niamh had a wise

23

look, an old head on young shoulders, Uncle Fergus called it.

The thought of an adventure clearly excited Niamh and Lucy as much as Jared. Was she the only one who was scared? Scared of what might happen. That they too would disappear and never come back, just like their…her…dad. On the other hand, it could all turn out to be nothing but a waste of time.

'I'm well up for sneaking out in the dark, spooky Halloween night,' whispered Jared, in a mock scary voice.

Tara was right; Jared shouldn't be going with them. He was never going to take this seriously. Say there was a gateway, what would he do then?

'…And wouldn't it be fun if we jumped through the gateway and had to fight terrible monsters,' he continued, 'and maybe even find a secret treasure map.'

Tara raised her eyebrows.

'W-well, at least sneaking out to pretend to go and do those things.' His ears lit up like beacons.

So he *was* hoping for more of an adventure. In a way, Tara was thankful, but she refused to let him know it. She couldn't help trying to knock him down a peg or two. 'Yeah, and we might get caught too? You know what your parents are like. You'll be grounded for the rest of the year.'

'True, but how much trouble can we get into? I mean we're only going to the end of your garden, right!'

'Not that much I suppose…' she was forced to admit.

'We *are* going to see the gateway though?' interjected Lucy, her big grey eyes, so like her brother's, looked earnestly at Tara as if she was just about to burst her bubble of excitement.

'Just think of it as a game, Lucy. We'll have fun,' said Tara, avoiding Jared's eyes at all costs. 'It's Halloween after all. It'll be spooky at the mound.' Lucy was so babyish – they shouldn't be taking her at all. Tara knew she'd be trouble, but it was too late to do anything about it now.

Tara looked at her watch, which signalled it was time to go.

Niamh went to her wardrobe and pulled out two backpacks.

'We packed some food, just in case.' She handed one of them to Jared and put the other over her shoulder.

Tara groaned, she didn't want Jared to think she actually believed there was gateway, just in case there wasn't. 'We'll have a midnight feast at the mound.'

'No we can't,' said Lucy. 'We need to keep it just in case we go through the gateway.'

Jared smirked.

'Shall we go, or are we to stand here chatting all night.' Tara spun around and led the way out of the door onto the landing.

They had just reached the stairs when Jared stood on a loose floorboard, which creaked loudly. They all froze. Tara stared at Jared, her eyes wide with anxiety in case anyone heard. Hopefully, Mum and Uncle Fergus would just think it was the house creaking and groaning as it settled for the night.

Lucy chuckled, and finding it hard to hold in her own laughter, Niamh put her hand over Lucy's mouth to stop her from making more noise. Tara bit hard on her lip to quell a nervous giggle. This was all so annoying. At this rate, they *would* be caught. Moving forward, she beckoned them on. Like four ghosts, they moved stealthily down the stairs and into the hall. They quietly rooted out their coats from under the stairs.

Tara indicated to the others to follow her into the kitchen. Once there, Tara closed the door and they all hurriedly put on their coats and jackets. She spotted her red scarf hanging over the back of a kitchen chair and wound it around her neck. Mum had knitted it, and Niamh had a similar one, which she now draped over her backpack.

'Do you have your torches ready,' whispered Jared.

Tara took hers out of her pocket and flicked it on and off to make sure it worked. Unlocking the old back door and locking it again after them, was a trial, as it made a terrible racket. After lots of shushing and grimacing, Tara finally achieved it.

Tara had another moment of doubt as the chill night air hit her and she saw the fingers of mist swirling about the garden. But what could possibly go wrong just a few metres from the house? They would either find the gateway or they would come straight back…simple. It was best not think of what might happen if they did find the gateway, and what they would actually do about it.

The mist began to cloak the full moon hanging like a huge globe in the navy-blue sky. Tara could still see a few stars twinkling in the clearer areas. A familiar smell of wood fires filled the air.

Jared grabbed the Jack-o'-Lantern off the windowsill, the candle in it still burning, and led the way.

Niamh and Lucy ran on ahead. Tara called them as loud as she dared, and she and Jared tried to keep up. How annoying, she should have known they'd do something like this. She ducked as something swooped over her head, and flinched as something scratched in the shadows. Bats and mice she reasoned, still she scuttled closer to Jared as they followed the cobblestone path more by feel than by sight. She could occasionally see the beams from Niamh and Lucy's torches flashing in and out of the pockets of fog. So at least they were okay.

To Tara's relief, they at last came to the field gate and climbed over it, making their way to the hawthorn trees.

'It's the witching hour,' Jared hissed in her ear, just as her torch went out, and she jumped as he shone his torch under his chin giving his face a spooky glow.

He laughed. 'You scared, Tara?'

'C-course not.' She could see he was going to be super annoying. She shook her torch and it came back on.

'Hmm, let's sneak up behind the others and scare them,' he said, smirking.

As they made their way around the mound, Tara just wanted to catch up with Niamh and Lucy and not be left alone with Jared. She wished he would walk faster not slower – it was slow going enough already with their feet sinking into the soggy earth. They had to watch they didn't stumble. Close to the mound, the ground dipped down into a shallow ditch, filled with mouldy leaves, giving off a rank smell of decay.

Tara could hear Niamh and Lucy muttering; only their voices never seemed to get any louder and it was beginning to be no fun at all.

On their side of the mound, the mist swirled eerily in small eddies over the Plain. Tara scurried past keeping her eyes fixed on Jared's back, resisting the urge to grab onto his coat. She was about to shout out for Niamh and Lucy to wait, not giving a fig about whether she was heard up at the house, when suddenly a bright blue flash of light lit up the back of the mound...then it was gone. Niamh and Lucy must have been in that same area and Tara hoped it didn't mean anything horrible.

Quickly, she pushed past Jared and made her way around the mound towards where she has seen the light flash. She suddenly tripped. Jared, right behind her when she stumbled, grabbed at her to stop her from falling and the Jack-o'-Lantern fell from his hand. She instantly understood why she had fallen, the ground beneath her feet trembled and a rumbling noise, like thunder, came from within the mound. She rocked backwards and forwards and her arms went out wide in an effort to keep her balance.

Shaking, she twisted towards Jared and another blue flash of light spread through the air, illuminating his astonished face.

Dropping her torch, Tara managed to grab both his arms as they both tumbled sideways. She lost her grip as a strong force lifted her from the ground, leaving her feet dangling in mid-air as she spun around and around.

Losing sight of Jared in the blueness of the mist, she twirled upwards. She screamed as an icy blast of air hit her in the face...

Chapter Three

Marvaanagh paced up and down the great chamber, her shoes click clacking on the stone floor. Clearly agitated, she rubbed the palms of her hands together, her long, slender fingers intertwining and an intense scowl putting lines around her handsome eyes.

A bang on the door reverberated around the walls, halting her in her tracks. Her scowl turned to an expression of pure rage.

'Enter!' she shouted.

There was a muttering as the door slowly opened, and a small, ugly and wretched creature, hobbled through, his eyes screwing up in an attempt to adjust to the darkness. His scaly tongue shot in and out of his mouth as he peered around to locate his mistress. She was standing next to the huge four-poster bed. The room had several large pieces of furniture, but only a couple of rugs to warm it up. A paltry fire burned in the inglenook fireplace. Zalen hated going in there, it was not just unwelcoming, but oppressive and threatening.

'Close the door, you feeble-minded spriggan! We must not be overheard.' Picking up her heavy black skirts, Marvaanagh swooped on him like a bat, her waist length ebony hair billowing on either side of her like wings.

Zalen turned to do her bidding, again muttering as he used his full weight to close the heavy oak door.

'A job half done is no job at all, spriggan!' roared Marvaanagh at his back. 'It was a simple task for most, yet you failed. Do you hear me...*failed!*'

Zalen jumped at this, almost trapping his fingers in the door. He half-turned to face her wrath. 'Mistress, of what do you speak? If it is to do with the stag...it was not my fault. S-someone left the gate open.'

Marvaanagh's eyes widened in rage, her voice booming

around the chamber: 'You let the stag *go!*'

Zalen gulped. Allowing the stag to escape obviously was not it. Many thoughts now flitted through his mind, and many a wrongdoing stopped for consideration, before he moved onto the next one, yet he found nothing that could cause the terrible fury of his mistress.

Marvaanagh's face grew crimson, ready to explode. 'The brat!' she yelled. She had moved closer to him and her spittle flecked his face.

Zalen shifted from one foot to the other, trying hard to keep his composure. She must mean the princess. But no, it could not be anything to do with her as he had just passed her on the way in. She had been sitting on a stone bench near the fountain playing with a kitten. Everything had appeared normal and she had even bestowed a pleasant smile on him, which was not so normal as it happened.

A horrific thought suddenly came thundering into his brain like a tidal wave. His mistress could not possibly mean the realm child, the one he changed! Many years had passed since he had taken her through the gateway and swapped her for the human child, but of course how dim-witted of him, he always knew it would one day come back to haunt him.

He had not liked being charged with the task of leaving a baby dead in the crib much as he hated children in general. But then he had not left her dead, and now she was returning. Long ago as it was, it had been a wretched night, and he shuddered at the memory of it. His hand drifted to his face and he ran his fingers over the ridges of the scars across his forehead and nose. He hoped he would never encounter the black fiend again. Then again, it had been nothing compared to facing his mistress when he had arrived back at her castle, Caer Searesby.

Marvaanagh pushed her face into his. 'The brat is planning her return,' she spat at him, confirming his suspicions. She continued her pacing of the chamber and Zalen waited, not daring to speak. 'Are you sure there was no sign of the bracelet when you dropped her in the crib.'

Zalen answered mechanically. 'None at all Mistress, it must have fallen off as we passed through the gateway.'

'The bracelet never leaves the wrist, unless the wearer is in the human world.'

'The same must happen within the gateway. I did search for it…but could find it nowhere. You can be assured it is lost forever in the twilight.' Zalen found it easy to lie – it was preferable to having his head chopped off. Anyway, for all he knew it could be it was lost. He thought it highly unlikely it would turn up again, and if that were the case, all would be well. If only the girl had stayed in the human world one more day, it would be out of his hands and no longer his problem.

'You are an idiot, spriggan, if you think for one moment I wish the bracelet to be lost forever. I *must* have it!' Marvaanagh hissed. 'Go forth immediately and travel the leys to the Vrogoly Gateway. It is the fastest and surest way. Try to get to that accursed child before she enters the gateway, for if she steps foot in the Realm of Wiltunscire she had better not be wearing the bracelet. Bring her back and I will deal with her, I refuse to leave it to you for a second time.'

'But mistress, it is most dangerous to travel the leys, I – I might be killed and then what use would I be. I am not like you. I do not have the secret to travel them safely—'

'You are right, spriggan.' Zalen took comfort that Marvaanagh was now very calm and controlled. 'But nor will you ever have the secret,' she continued, her voice rising, 'and if you do not bring back the bracelet and the girl, you are as good as dead anyway! So you have *nothing* to lose!'

Two seconds later Zalen was out of the room, best not to linger, he decided. Travelling the ley tunnels was his only option. If only he knew his mistress's protection spell. She was the only person in the three realms that held the knowledge of safely travelling the leys. But he had to get to the Vrogoly Gateway as it was the only way into the human world this night, just as it was on that fateful night so many years before.

The gateways only opened at certain times of the day or year, and every gateway was different. The Vrogoly Gateway was unusual in that it only opened once a year, this very night, Samhain, a magical time in the human world. On this evening, the veil between the worlds thinned and folk could pass either way through the gateway.

If he was to be on time to catch up with the girl as she came through it, he had no choice but to go by ley. One day though, he would find the secret of travelling them safely, then, he would not only be free, but powerful too. Everyone would be seeking his services, and the price would be high.

Zalen headed out of the castle and down to where the five rivers met. Every inch of the way took him back to that night, many years before. He arrived all too soon at the gateway, quivering with fear, his heartbeat drumming in his ears.

Nothing could protect him from what lay ahead, so he thought it best not to ponder on it. He took a deep gulp of air and stepped into the middle of the oak, ash and hawthorn trees. Instantly a force struck him so hard, he jumped back out again, every inch of him quivering. The memory of the last journey arose stark in his mind. Maybe he should just make his escape while he could, travel the snail way along the roads to the Realm of Dumnonia where his family lived and beg their forgiveness. Deep down, he knew he would not get very far as Marvaanagh would catch up with him in no time. There was no way out, Marvaanagh had him trapped and it was his own fault.

Positioning himself for the impact, for the first time in many years, he stepped once more into the centre of the trees.

Chapter Four

Someone shook Tara. 'Wake up! Wake up!' a voice cried. It was Jared's, somewhere in the distance.

'Wake up!'

The voice sounded nearer now and Tara could hear birds singing their dawn chorus. She slowly opened her eyes. Broad daylight blinded her. She squinted up at a cloudless, lavender sky with the shimmering sun warming her face. She closed her eyes again in an attempt to clear the fog from her head. They'd been trying to catch up to Niamh and Lucy. There had been a terrible flash of light. She didn't remember anything else. Tentatively, she opened her eyes again to see Jared's bewildered face looming over her, blocking out the sun.

'What's going on,' she said, anxious now as she struggled to sit up.

'Look!' cried Jared, kneeling over her and shaking her again.

'Stop shaking me!' He let go and she sat up.

'Wow, can't believe this!' Jared said in utter astonishment. 'Where are we?'

Tara ran her fingertips over the dew soaked grass. Afraid to look around at first, she forced herself to look up and saw they sat high up in a vivid green, rolling landscape of lush meadow, strewn with copper-red and sunset-orange tinted trees and bushes. Oak, beech and sweet chestnut trees, swaying in the pleasant breeze, whispered together in groups as if discussing the situation. Nestling further downhill was a forest.

The gigantic morning sun was clearing a few leftover pockets of mist from the dips and gullies below them, revealing the glistening, silver river, winding merrily down into the valley.

They had landed in an unworldly place of vivid colour overhung with an eerie calmness. Tara swallowed hard. 'The Otherworld, the land of the fae.'

'You're joking! I can't believe it.'

'Okay...what's your explanation then?'

'I don't mean literally joking, you ninny. We obviously came through the gateway. I mean all the spinning around and blue light. Where else could we be? Unless someone knocked us out and is playing a trick. And somehow I don't think so. But until we see something weird we can't know for sure.'

Tara shut her eyes in the struggle to remember what happened, then opened them wide, at the same time reaching out and grabbing Jared's arms. 'Where are Niamh and Lucy?'

Jared shrugged. 'Maybe they haven't come through the gateway yet.'

'They must have, before we saw the flash we had already seen a flash of light around the back of the mound. They must have come here just before us. We need to find them!'

Scrambling to her feet, Tara shook her stiff limbs. Her body ached and she realised she had a few bruises. She checked her watch – it had stopped. She tapped it several times – it refused to work.

Scanning the area she was surprised to see the mound sitting behind them, but there was no house – no village in the distance. Her torch and the extinguished Jack o'Lantern lay on the grass. Tara bent down and picked up her torch, putting into her coat pocket. Her head whipped around as she thought she saw something out of the corner of her eye, but there was nothing there.

Startled, she heard loud neighing and whinnying. The ground vibrated beneath their feet. In the distance, a cloud of dust moved towards them, there was a dull thundering sound. It wasn't until the cloud came nearer that Tara saw a herd of wild horses racing towards them across the landscape.

She and Jared, both began to walk backwards up the slope not taking their eyes off the herd. A tremor of terror rippled through Tara and the familiar icy prickles ran up her arms as they came closer. So close in fact, she could see their flared nostrils and smelt their hot sweaty smell as they passed, then they were gone, the thundering hooves retreating into silence.

'Wow!' said Jared. 'That was close.'

'Just wild horses,' said Tara with a nonchalance she didn't feel. 'Is that weird enough for you?'

Sounds of whispering came from behind her. Tara nervously whipped around, but spotted nothing except for a backpack up by the mound. It looked like the one Jared had been carrying so she strode over to it. No sooner had she picked it up when a swarm of small, ugly and bizarrely dressed men and women, came scampering from behind the mound. They scurried around her legs, garbling in a strange language, not one of them was more than knee high.

Tara yelled out, frightened by their large bulbous heads, bulging eyes and hooked noses. Before Jared reached her side, one jumped up, snatched the backpack from her hands and tore it apart. He emptied the contents onto the ground, which the others immediately jumped on. They scrabbled, squabbled and fought each other for the cakes and sandwiches, which littered the grass.

'Hey you lot, that's *our* food!' cried Jared.

One of the little men whipped around, snarling and hissing. To Tara's astonishment, his forehead began to grow to enormous proportions. Her feet took root as she stared at once fascinated and terrified as his arms and legs stretched like thick elastic, his stomach swelled out of his trousers, bare and hairy, his finger-nails growing hooked like an eagle's talons.

In a few seconds, he stood high above them towering like a giant. He glared menacingly down and with one swipe of his enormous sledgehammer hand, sent Jared rolling down the hill.

As the giant turned towards her, he gave Tara a perfunctory glance and obviously not seeing her as a threat, quickly shrank to his previous size and carried on scavenging in the grass.

Tara spun around and sprinted down the slope after Jared. By the time she reached him, he'd stopped rolling and lay flat on his face. Grabbing his coat, she attempted to haul him to his feet. 'Get up! Get up!'

'I'm all right by the way, just a few bruises.' He struggled to his feet, wiping his hands on his coat, but all that did was make them wetter.

'Oh, shut up and run!'

'Where do we go?'

'I don't know, just run.'

Ahead of them, a great white stag emerged from the forest. It stood on a pathway facing in their direction. Turning it ran back into the trees.

'We can hide there,' said Jared.

Without looking behind them, they ran until they reached the forest path, at last Tara turned, but no one followed. She stopped to catch her breath. Bending down she put her hands on her knees and leant on them. Jared had run on ahead, but now stopped, realising she wasn't following. He turned. Seeing the scared expression on his face and realising she must look the same, Tara blushed and quickly straightened up.

'Who in the name of Mrs Twigge's big nose were they?' asked Jared.

Mrs Twigge was their maths teacher, but Tara didn't feel like laughing. 'I don't know, but I hope we never see them again.'

'Well now, that's what *I* call weird, now I'm convinced we're in the Otherworld.'

Tara looked ahead of them – the white stag trotted on down the path. What now? She sucked in her breath, shrugged at Jared and began to follow it, what other choice did they have?

Walking on a thick carpet of golden and russet fallen leaves, Tara took in her surroundings. The autumn sun filtered through the trees revealing a kaleidoscope of vibrant red, burnished gold, flaming orange and jade. The breeze swayed the boughs, sending large leaves floating through the air like golden snow. A lovely earthy, woodsy smell invoked happy memories for Tara of the family working together to gather up the damp fallen leaves, which littered the garden every autumn. If anyone saw them, they would think they were just taking a pleasant walk in the woods. But they weren't. They didn't know where they were, where Niamh and Lucy were, or what lay ahead. Thinking about it now, Tara realised they hadn't thought this out at all, what they would do if they did pass through the gateway, because they – she – had doubted the truth of the story.

Unsure if they were doing the right thing, but sensing there was no immediate danger, Tara felt they had no choice, but to continue along the path. Where else could they go? She had no wish to go back, that was for sure. Further on, the stag stopped, looked back at them and walked into the undergrowth. He took a few steps, backed out again and continued onwards.

'What was all that about?' asked Tara. She quickened her pace; hoping Niamh and Lucy were there in the trees. She reached the place where the stag had stopped and spotted something red lying in the bracken. Hurrying over, she pulled it out. Turning to Jared, she laughed with relief. 'They came this way. This is Niamh's scarf, she must have dropped it.'

'See I was right to say we should come this way,' boasted Jared.

'We need to walk faster,' said Tara, ignoring his remark, she was certainly not going to agree with him.

'I'm starving though. It must be way past breakfast time.'

'*Eating* is not a priority right now,' said Tara haughtily. Why did boys always have to think about food, it was so annoying?

'It's my *only* priority right now.' Jared's stomach rumbled loudly just to prove his point.

'Then all the more reason to catch up with Niamh and Lucy, they have the other backpack.'

'Okay, *Mum!*'

Tara gritted her teeth, spun around, and marched onwards.

Tara had lost track of time, they'd been walking for ages in silence. Jared must have sensed her mood, as he hadn't tried speaking to her. She'd felt sure they should have caught up to Niamh and Lucy by now. What kept niggling at her was why they hadn't waited for her and Jared to wake up too. Why go on alone? Had the small people jumped out on them and made them run? Or had they for some reason not seen her and Jared when they woke up, possibly because they landed somewhere else or even worse, someone had kidnapped them! What she couldn't bear to think of was that Niamh and Lucy had deliberately gone off without them, but she supposed it to be the most likely explanation. This riled her and she walked faster still, determined to catch up, her anger spurring her on.

The stag had vanished from sight. It grew darker as the oak branches created a canopy overhead, cutting out the sunlight, the path narrowing as they made their way deeper into the forest.

Jared tripped on a hidden tree root. 'Whoops,' he said and laughed.

It broke the tension, Tara couldn't help but grin, and it prompted Jared to speak. 'What d'you think is happening back home?'

Tara had been avoiding thinking about it. It was only a short time since they'd left their homes…wasn't it? 'I don't know,' she said. 'Do you think it's daylight back home too?'

'Dunno, maybe…maybe not.' Jared shrugged his shoulders. 'Anyway, there's not much we can do about it, so maybe we should get on with finding Lucy and Niamh, then I can eat.'

'It was *you* who brought the subject up,' Tara reminded him. She dug her knuckles into his arm.

Jared retaliated by pulling her hair. Tara grabbed a handful of large oak leaves and flung them at him. She darted along the winding path and finding a spiky, green chestnut case turned and hurled that at him too. Jared picked it up, throwing it back. She ducked and it missed, hitting an enormous old oak tree to the side of her.

'Ha ha,' teased Tara.

'Be careful, *humans*,' said a melodious voice.

Tara jumped in alarm, holding her breath, and Jared ran over just in time to see a shadowy figure begin to peel itself from the oak. Perfectly camouflaged, for a moment it appeared the figure was part of the tree. Tara recoiled as it stepped out onto the path. She let out her breath as she could see it was most definitely a girl.

Chapter Five

The girl stood separate from the tree. She was older than Tara and Jared, but smaller, standing at about five feet tall. Her long, flowing dress was varying shades of brown, the folds of which resembled spiky leaves. Her skin was tawny, and her piercing eyes, hazel. While staring intently at Jared, she played with her rust-coloured wild hair, which fell around her shoulders like tangled tree roots.

Tara stood transfixed. She'd never seen anyone who looked like this before – there was something sinister about the girl. A feeling of dread came over her. She had often sensed when a situation wasn't right, though not as strongly as she did now. Reaching over, she patted Jared's arm to try to alert him.

The girl saw her and Tara noticed the expression in her piercing eyes turn fleetingly sly. 'I am Sylvia...the spirit of this tree,' she said, addressing Jared directly, her voice hauntingly soft. The sly look rapidly vanished as she coyly cast down her eyes. 'And who are you, human? What is your business here in Vrogoly Forest?' She raised her chin again as she spoke managing to captivate Jared's admiring eyes, which now fixed firmly on her own.

'H-hi, I-I'm Jared, and er...this is Tara. Have you seen two girls pass this way?'

Tara's hand was still on Jared's arm, she squeezed it again, but there was no reaction. He seemed hypnotised. Tara had never seen him act this way before – lost for words. She supposed Sylvia was pretty in an unusual way. Her cheekbones were high, her face heart-shaped and her chin came to a small point. An odd face as far as Tara was concerned, and it matched her manner. There was something shifty about her for sure.

'I may be able to help you,' Sylvia said in lilting tones. 'Please come into my home and we shall discuss this further.'

Tara instinctively bristled at this suggestion. They shouldn't trust her...they didn't know her. This could be a trick to lure them somewhere. In their own world, they wouldn't go into a strange home, so here in the Otherworld they should surely not even think about it. 'Can you please tell us whether or not you've seen two girls pass this way?' she insisted, curtly, but politely. 'We can't stop as we *need* to find them.'

Sylvia kept her focus on Jared and addressing Tara without looking at her, she said, 'Your friend wants to come in. You do not have to.

'Yes, I want to go in,' Jared agreed. 'Maybe Sylvia can tell us what we need to know.'

'If you will come this way,' said Sylvia. 'I will do my best to help.'

'Thank you, we will.' Jared nodded his head vigorously.

A blush steadily grew, starting in Tara's cheeks, before spreading down through her neck and chest. At the same time, the anger welled up from her stomach until she was fit to burst. 'Jar-ed!' she cried.

Sylvia smiled deviously as she turned and placed both hands on the tree. It gradually became transparent, revealing a doorway. She stepped inside, gesturing for them to follow. Tara tightened her grip on Jared's arm. Without a word, Jared pulled away from her and stepped through the doorway.

Tara hesitated outside, fearful of Sylvia trapping them inside the tree. But Jared was already in there, so she had no choice. She walked through and with a flash of inspiration, dropped Niamh's scarf half in and half out of the doorway just as it began to fade. Well, at least now she knew exactly where the doorway was.

Tara had entered a cosy home, much larger than the outside of the tree. The strong scent of pine tickled her nose, and strings of fir cones and acorns decorated the circular walls. In the centre, three comfortable wooden chairs with green cushions surrounded a low table on which was standing an oil lamp and a vase of pine and conifer branches. Through a small archway and down a step, Tara spied a quaint bed, with a silken green cover. The smell of fresh bread drifted by, and Tara followed it to see a loaf of crusty bread, cheese and a large milk jug standing on a small table on the other side of the room. Jared was eyeing them hungrily.

'Do take off your outer garments and make rest,' said Sylvia, her melodious voice hypnotic.

Jared took off his coat and sat down, his eyes still fixed on the food. Tara slammed herself down in a seat, leaving her coat on and folded her arms across her chest. She noticed the doorway had completely gone and shuddered. The only light came from the lamp and higher up the tree from a small hole. The rough bark of the walls, closed in on them like a prison cell.

'What are you doing in *my* world, human...Jared?' asked Sylvia, again focusing her attention purely on him.

'As we said already,' Tara interrupted, annoyed that Sylvia continued to ignore her, 'we're searching for my sister...I mean our sisters. They're somewhere here in *your* world. They're both eleven years old. Now, have you seen them or not?'

'There's no need to be so crabby, Tara,' said Jared, frowning. 'Sylvia's only trying to help us.'

Tara felt the blood rush to her face, how could Jared be so blind? Sylvia turned to look at Tara, and confidently smiled, not even trying to hide the deceitfulness in her expression. She was letting Tara know she had no control over the situation.

Tara's stomach churned. Beads of perspiration broke out on her forehead and her heart thumped wildly. They should never have come inside. She should have insisted they travel on. Taking a deep breath to try to quell her panic, she said, 'Our sisters will be looking for a human girl, who'd be about eleven years old too. Do you know of any humans? A girl with straw-berry-blonde hair who is possibly with a human man? If you don't, we have to be on our way or our sisters will get too far ahead of us.'

Sylvia turned her full attention now to Tara. She smiled at her. 'I am most sorry, but I do not know of any such humans.' Sylvia's gaze continued to hold hers, and Tara found she couldn't tear her eyes away. She wriggled uncomfortably in her chair until Sylvia's self-satisfied expression goaded her into defiantly staring back. Tara could outstare anyone. Even Niamh couldn't beat her at it. One of the ways she achieved this was to let her mind wander to other things and this she did. She kept her eyes steady, looking right through Sylvia's glacial stare.

Before long, Tara knew she was winning as Sylvia's eyes softened and Tara was no longer afraid. The scent of the pine grew cloying and intoxicating and soon everything took on a dreamlike quality. She relaxed back in her chair and let the tension drain out of her knotted muscles.

She concentrated on what lay ahead, yes, they would have to move on shortly and find Niamh and Lucy before they got too far away. Hunger gnawed at her stomach. They could eat something as soon as they caught up with them, no way would she touch Sylvia's food. She yawned, the light affecting her eyes making it impossible to keep them open. Rubbing at them and rapidly blinking, she tried to open them, but they stung so much she had to close them again.

Sleepiness overcoming her, again she tried in vain to open her eyes, only her eyelids stuck like glue, her arms weighing heavily on the arms of the chair. Her normal thoughts gradually drifted into an unfathomable chasm somewhere deep in her mind. She sank down, down, down.

Somebody tapped her hand, a sharp, stinging tap that was most annoying. Tara wished they would stop. Through the swirling fuzziness of her sleep, she could hear a voice faintly calling to her. Uncle Fergus's face loomed up into her mind, an intense frown wrinkling his forehead. 'Time to wake up Tara,' he said sharply. 'That's a good girl.' This time Tara heard him loud and clear. Sleepily, she smiled, wanting to turn over and go back to sleep, but he gave her an *it's time to get up right now* sort of look. Tara struggled to obey; she didn't want to annoy Uncle Fergus.

She fought to open her eyes. It was too difficult, but Uncle Fergus kept calling…telling her to wake up. She was so tired and just wanted to sleep. Uncle Fergus, his eyebrows knitted together, stubbornly stayed there. She tried again and put all the effort she could muster into it. At last, she floated up into awareness, her startled eyes shooting open as once more she became alert. They were in danger!

Sylvia looked briefly bewildered before scowling petulantly. Jared was sitting back in his chair nonchalantly examining the room.

'You must have come through the Vrogoly Gateway, I believe, to gain access to this world,' said Sylvia, bringing her mock sweet voice back into play. 'Perhaps your sisters did not come through with you.'

Jared yawned. 'You could be right there.'

'That couldn't be true, Jared!' protested Tara, regaining her fight. She stood up. 'There was the blue light, remember, and we found Niamh's scarf.'

'Tara, just listen to Sylvia.' Jared's expression glazed over, he was speaking, but wasn't there at all. What had Sylvia done? Jared knew Niamh and Lucy were in the Otherworld too. Had she already enchanted him in some way?

Tara took a deep breath to calm herself and said as firmly as possible, 'Jared, it's dangerous here, we're leaving right now.'

Sylvia turned to Jared. 'You are tired. I suggest you rest here for a while. Afterwards, you will be in a better frame of mind to make decisions.'

Jared yawned. 'Actually, funnily enough, I do feel tired…very…very tired.' He yawned again. 'Sit down Tara, I don't know about you, but I could do with having a quick nap.'

A satisfied smile abruptly softened Sylvia's features. Jared sank even further back in his chair and fell instantly asleep. Sylvia must have charmed him just as she had tried to charm her.

Tara moved swiftly to his chair. 'Wake up, Jared,' she shouted shaking him. There was no movement and once more the panic welled up inside her. 'Wake up! Fight the sleepiness Jared! We have to get out of here.'

Tara ran to where the scarf poked out of the doorway. She put her hands on the bark and tried to open it as she had seen Sylvia do, but nothing happened. She ran back to Jared and shook him – still no response, not even a flicker of an eyelid. Tara turned and stared at Sylvia who gave her a knowing smile.

Sylvia went to the wall and placed her hands on it. The doorway reopened with ease. She waved Tara out. 'Go, I will take care of him.' She moved calmly to the side table and began to prepare food.

Tara stared at her back. She couldn't, wouldn't leave Jared. Turning her attention back to him, she tried to drag him up. He was a dead weight. With both hands she grabbed his jumper and shook him vigorously, his head dropped limply onto the arm of the chair. How could he have been so stupid? What should she do? She had no choice...she *had* to go. She must find Niamh and Lucy, come back for Jared later.

Looking at Jared in despair she marched through the door, tears of frustration running down her face. She stopped outside. 'As soon as I've found them, I'll come back for Jared,' she shouted. 'You can't keep him here!'

Sylvia carried on with what she was doing, her back to Tara, choosing to pay no heed. The door faded away and Tara was alone.

Chapter Six

The two girls lay under the birch tree on a bed of faded golden leaves, where Zalen had placed them a few hours earlier. From behind a huge copper beech opposite, he watched the scene with impatience. The sun had risen some time ago and it was not safe to be hanging around. His mistress would be wondering where he was. He should have returned by now. Why did they not wake up? Then he remembered humans seldom rose with the growing light anymore.

He stared at the bracelet sparkling on one girl's arm, he had tried to take it, but now she had returned to the Realm of Wiltunscire, it would not budge. Queen Marvaanagh would never forgive this, he could not go back to Caer Searesby, but going back to his own people and hoping they would accept and protect him was also not an option.

Many years ago, he had betrayed them back in the Realm of Dumnonia, by stealing the map that led to the secret island, Ynys Is. Marvaanagh had promised him great riches in return for the map. Believing her, he had carried out all her biddings without question. She had lied of course, keeping him with her by fear and with threats she would tell his people he was responsible for taking the map. He had tried to get it back, but to no avail.

Now he was alone, without family, without friends, without anyone. He sighed. No, the only option was to seek help from someone who would find this momentous event very interesting, in fact, very interesting indeed. He might even make a little gold out of it.

Zalen found it hard to stay awake and keep his wits about him. Battered and bruised from travelling the ley, he had been up all night and in pain. Having to move the two younger girls away from the older two human children and into the forest had taken the last of his strength. Having the ability to shape shift had made it easier, and one trip was all he needed, but that was all his remaining energy spent. It was worth it though as it would be less of a problem to deal with two children than four, and the older two might be tricky, especially the boy, but there was something he recognised in the girl too, something he did not much like.

At last the realm child stirred. She sat up. Zalen watched, as rubbing her eyes with her knuckles, she tried to make sense of what she saw. She turned to the other girl and shook her awake.

'What's happening, what's the matter!' the human girl cried, and abruptly sat up. She vigorously rubbed her eyes too. 'Where are we? No...we can't have...gosh we did, we did! We went through the gateway. I remember now. We're here, aren't we?'

'Yes,' said the realm child. 'We're really here, we must be!'

'But where's Jared, and – and Tara?'

'They must be here somewhere.'

Zalen decided to make his move. He stepped out from behind the tree.

'Do not be alarmed,' he assured them. It was too late, the human girl let out a high-pitched squeal. Sometimes he wished he were a little more personable in looks. He tried to keep his tongue from shooting out of his mouth too much.

'I am Zalen, I am a friend. I am here only to help you, not to hurt you in any way. But I must tell you both, you are in grave danger.' The human girl snivelled and tried to pull the other one back towards the trees.

'Shh, Lucy, it's okay,' said the realm child. She stared at him, not appearing to be too troubled by his appearance. 'Who are you and how do you know we're in danger?'

'I am a servant at Caer Searesby, a castle which is further south in this realm.' The two girls stared at each other nonplussed. Zalen continued, 'I overheard a conversation. There are those who knew you were coming through the gateway. Your arrival here will upset a great many people. Those people wish you only harm. I am here to offer you assistance.'

'*They* knew we were coming?' questioned the realm child. 'Who are *they*? We didn't tell anyone, did we, Lucy?'

The other girl heartily shook her head. 'No, Niamh, I didn't tell anyone, only Jared.'

At last he knew her name. He needed it to gain her trust. He had to win her over somehow if his plan was to work. The long night had given him plenty of time to think. He was too late to take the bracelet and his mistress would see that as unforgivable. Failing once, with a valid excuse, he might get away with. But failing twice with no excuse and also revealing he lied about what happened the first time, well in his mistress's eyes it would be unforgiveable. His life would end unless he did something to save himself.

'There are eyes in the human world,' he said. 'They have been watching you, Niamh. Waiting for you.' Zalen watched the girl's expression. She did not appear afraid, but the human girl stood behind her sniffing loudly.

'Do *they* know who I am, these people? Do *you* know who I am…where I come from?' As she said this, she pointed to herself and the bracelet on her arm glistened in the early morning sunshine.

Icy fingers played tunes on Zalen's vertebrae as he recalled those indigo baby eyes staring up at him all those years ago, and how close he came to wiping out their sparkle. Taking a deep breath he said calmly, 'No, but I believe you are of royal blood. Only someone of erm…royal blood would wear such a bracelet.' The girls exchanged glances and giggled, they obviously thought something he said was funny…how annoying. He forced himself to stay calm. 'Someone took you to the human world when you were a baby. You are a changeling.'

'A changeling!' The realm child looked excited.

Zalen knew he had her attention. He ventured, 'You were exchanged for another child—'

'I know…well, we thought so. Where is the other baby, erm, I mean girl, now?'

'I do not know,' he lied. 'However, I know someone who can tell you more. We must hurry…move away from the danger and make our way to Vrogoly Palace.' He lifted his head, but kept his manner subservient. 'Princess Gwyn I am sure will help you.'

'*Princess!*' The human girl called Lucy now stepped forward clearly impressed by this news. She grabbed at the realm child's arm.

'First, where are we? What's this place called again?' asked Niamh.

Zalen bowed so deeply his head touched his knees. 'The Realm of Wiltunscire…and I am your servant.'

Both the girls giggled. Zalen hated having to bow to two silly girls, but at least he had their attention. He had to get them to go with him. His mistress would already be searching for them, which meant getting them away from here as quickly as possible.

'We can't go anywhere without Jared and Tara,' insisted the girl Lucy.

Zalen predicted this and he was ready with his next lie. This was why he had moved the other children. 'You have been here at the entrance to the gateway for many hours and as you can see…your friends did not make it through in time.'

'They're not our friends,' said Lucy. 'It's my brother and Niamh's sister. Are you sure they didn't come through?'

Zalen ignored the human girl, she was of no importance, and addressed Niamh. With her folded arms and furrowed brow, she was not quite as sure of herself as she appeared. He used it to his advantage. 'I am sure. As you can see, they are not here. We must move on and with great haste to the Princess Gwyn, you will be safe with her. It is imperative we keep moving.'

'I don't want to be here without Jared,' cried Lucy.

'I don't like being here without Tara either, Lucy,' replied Niamh. 'But now we *are* here, we need to find someone to help us.'

'Okay, Niamh, but I'm scared.'

Niamh turned to Zalen. 'Would this Princess Gwyn know anything about a human man? We think he came here too. He's my dad, well sort of my dad...actually, I suppose he never was...'

She trailed off, confusion causing her dark brows to meet across her forehead, immediately reminding him of someone else he knew well. It would be useless hiding her ancestry as she looked too much like the rest of her family. Yet, it would be foolish to tell them everything. He still might have a chance to get out of this mess. Princess Gwyn herself would not know anything for certain. She would only be able to make guesses. Acting ignorant was his best bet.

'If anyone knows anything, it will be the princess.'

The two girls looked at each other. 'All right,' agreed Niamh, obviously at a loss as to what else to do. 'How far is it?'

'It is quite some distance away, across the river on the other side of the forest. It will take some hours to get there.' Probably more he thought, with his body so battered by travelling the leys, yes, it would be slow going. 'We will stay on the path for a short while, then make our way through the thick of the forest on a hidden path. It will be safer that way.'

He twisted painfully around and began to hobble onwards down the path. Yes, it would be slow going indeed.

'Come with me or stay as you please,' he called behind him, knowing now they would choose to follow.

Chapter Seven

Tara stood staring at the coarse bark of the tree, wishing she hadn't left and wondering with horror how she would get back in again when she needed to. Anger spurred her on and she dashed the tears from her cheeks with the back of her hand. She would have to go and find the others.

She scrutinised the area. With so many great old oaks in the forest, she needed to remember which one this was.

Glancing down, Tara spied Niamh's scarf peeping from beneath the trunk, half in and half out of the invisible doorway. She couldn't be sure Sylvia wouldn't spot it. The tree was very old indeed, all gnarled and knobbly. Sprinkled around it was an abundance of mushrooms – red with white spots. Tara recognised them as the *fly agaric*. Uncle Fergus had warned them that although they may look pretty, they were poisonous.

A quick hunt confirmed none lay around any other oak in the area. Searching upwards into the branches of golden leaves, she spotted a ball of green mistletoe hanging there. She stored the picture of it in her head until she was satisfied she would recognise the tree again even amidst the other old oaks.

Tara viewed the path ahead with trepidation. Narrowing, it looked gloomy and the forest canopy became even denser, with hardly any daylight shining through the crowded boughs. The leaves were mushy underfoot and smelt of mildew. Decaying tree trunks littered the sides of the path.

She pulled her scarf tighter around her neck, covering any bare skin, and pushed one hand deep into her pocket to protect it, from what, she didn't know exactly. From the other pocket she took her torch. Its light brought her some comfort and briskly she trudged onwards, focusing on her feet. At this moment, she'd rather be anywhere, but here on her own.

A resounding crack echoed in the silence as Tara trod on a

twig snapping it. Something flew out in front of her with a great flapping. Screeching she brought her hands up to shield her face. Quickly seeing it was a grouse taking its noisy flight, didn't cause her to feel any calmer, her heart beat a military tattoo in her chest. 'Phew,' she said aloud, her voice sounding strange to her. She took a deep breath to try to slow her heartbeat. She would have to try to develop some – what was it Uncle Fergus called it – mettle…yes that was it, mettle. He always said Niamh had more than her fair share of it. Well she wished Niamh was here with her right now, sharing it with her.

Plodding onwards, Tara's thoughts drifted back to the oak tree. Uncle Fergus had somehow helped her fight against Sylvia. She didn't know why he had popped up in her head like that. She tried not to think what would have happened if Sylvia had managed to charm her too. It was too horrible to think about. This Otherworld was a dangerous place to be, and the fae folk she'd always imagined to be friendly, were tricky if Sylvia was anything to go by. Somewhere in the forest, Niamh and Lucy walked alone and anything could have happened to them.

Suddenly, something howled in the distance, jerking Tara to a halt. She held her breath as fear engulfed her. Her head tucked into her shoulders, she glanced fearfully around and shone her torchlight into the forest undergrowth. The light fell on what looked suspiciously like brown fur concealed in the bracken. Her legs turned to jelly. Not waiting to find out what it was, she ran, not really watching where she was going or even to care about it. She ran until her legs ached and her breathing hurt her chest.

At last the canopy of trees thinned, shafts of sunlight fanned through them illuminating her way, which Tara found reassuring and she slowed her pace. Tall, slender, silver birch edged the path, their autumn gold branches drooping low. She put her torch back into her pocket. How far away must Niamh and Lucy be by now? Surely they couldn't have got that far. She couldn't go on much longer as anything could be happening back at

Sylvia's oak, but the idea of returning on her own through the dark part of the forest, for the time being, kept her moving. She hoped Jared would continue to sleep for a good while, as Tara couldn't bear to think what other bewitchments Sylvia would place on him now she had him alone.

She hurried onwards, her eyes darting from side to side hoping to spot Niamh and Lucy. It was a few minutes before she noticed it had gone eerily quiet. She couldn't even hear the rustling of a leaf or a tweet from a bird.

A ghostly whistling sound came from within the trees and as the sound became louder and louder, it took a moment for Tara to realise it sounded just like wind gusting down a chimney.

As it came howling ominously closer, it caught up leaves from the ground blowing them furiously about her. A patch of mist formed in front of her and Tara anxiously glanced around to see where she could run to and hide. She had hardly taken a step backwards when out of the mist materialised a hare. Horrified, she recognised it as the one from the mound. Its mustard eyes glowed just like before.

Tara cried out as it began to spin. The mist swirled around with it into a vortex, whipping up more leaves from the ground. She tried to step away, but the force of it pulled her forward, drawing her in.

Suddenly, a flash of white bore down on her from her left side. The hare abruptly stopped spinning and Tara fell to the ground with a painful bump. She looked up to see the white stag. He put down his head, his great antlers poised in a threatening position, his hooves tramping the ground. And just like at the mound when the raven appeared, the hare leapt up and turning in the air, dashed off into the forest leaving her alone with the stag.

Tara stared at him. Was he planning to hurt her? She sat stock still, not daring to move a muscle. The stag lifted his head, nodded at her, then calmly walked back into the forest.

Once he was out of sight, Tara struggled to her feet and ran, her eyes fixed on the path ahead. The hare without doubt meant to harm her in some way. What did it want of her? Was it trying to frighten her away, or even worse? But she appeared to have gained a friend too, the stag. If he hadn't come along right then, she dreaded to think what might have happened. Still, among the trees and undergrowth, she could sense eyes upon her...the hare...the stag?

Just ahead, the path widened into a small glade, Tara was heartened. Maybe Niamh and Lucy were there.

She quickened her steps, her eyes frantically searching the area. She was afraid to call out in case she alerted anyone or anything. Then a strange feeling overwhelmed her...a good feeling. The birch trees had given way to chestnut and copper beech, but in the middle of the glade stood an elder tree, with bunches of shrivelled purple berries hanging among its golden leaves.

Tara spotted a movement behind the twisted trunk and her heart racing with joy she flew around it expecting to see Niamh and Lucy. There was no one there. She looked down and realised she had stepped into the middle of a ring of toadstools, which sat on a perfect circle of lush grass. She recognised it as a fairy ring as she had seen one before. Uncle Fergus has told her and Niamh they shouldn't step in them or the fae folk could enchant them.

A melodic tinkling attracted her attention, something familiar about it reminded Tara of her mother's musical box, which played a lullaby when opened. It was a comforting sound. Tara looked up to see several women approaching her through the trees. They wore beautiful, white, delicate dresses that sparkled in the autumn sunshine like spider webs, their long golden hair wreathed with flowers, ribbons and small silver bells. Tara realised the tinkling noise was their laughing voices.

They skipped towards her, their feet gliding over the ground. Their beauty captivated her and she impulsively held out her hands to them. Skipping into the ring, they encircled her, taking her hands and pulling her around into a dance. Joyfully she joined in. She heard herself laughing, her own voice sounding as sweet as theirs. It delighted her and she laughed louder.

The woman next to Tara took her own circlet of flowers and placed it on her hair and at the same time Tara's clothes faded away and she looked down to see she was wearing a flowing white gossamer dress. As she danced the dress floated around her like flower petals. Mesmerised by it, a feeling of serenity and elation filtered through her, she no longer cared about anything, just the compulsive urge to dance. The women on either side of her smiled their encouragement as she twirled around never wanting to stop.

Unexpectedly the branches of the elder tree opened to reveal sitting among them a petite old woman, her rich chestnut hair streaked with grey. She wore a dress of moss green from which more shrivelled elderberries hung. The women stopped dancing, the tinkling stopped and the wonderful feeling ebbed away. Tara was filled with dread...another tree spirit; she hoped the dancing women would protect her. But when she turned to them, they had vanished.

'Do not be afraid, little one,' said the woman kindly. 'I am Hylda the mother of this tree. You ought to be more careful, it is so easy to find yourself caught up in something like the beautiful dancing and forget who you are and why you are here. Perhaps it would be wise to step out of the ring.'

Tara thought for a second. Yes, she did forget. It was as if she was one of the women and could have danced forever not caring about anything or anyone. How silly of her to be caught up again in a charm, just like Jared. She bit on her lip and stepped out of the ring, her gossamer dress vanished, and once more she wore her own clothes. Removing the circlet of flowers from her hair, she threw it down in disgust.

'No matter, you are safe now,' said Hylda. 'Who are you and what do you seek?'

'I-I'm Tara, and I'm looking for my sister,' she said, still not quite sure if Hylda was entirely trustworthy. She did her best to appear friendly, even though her throat tightened with apprehension. 'She's here somewhere with her friend Lucy. I need to find them quickly. Lucy's brother is trapped in the home of a tree spirit called Sylvia.'

'Ah, Sylvia, the dryad of the ancient oak,' Hylda said thoughtfully. 'A quiet girl. Hmm…normally keeps herself to herself.'

'Yes that's right, it was an ancient oak. I think Jared is in danger. He fell asleep and wouldn't—' she corrected herself, 'couldn't, come with me! He didn't fall asleep by himself, Sylvia made him. She tried to do the same to me.'

'Goodness. *Really?*'

'Yes, really, I'm sure he would have come with me. I think he's under a spell. He's looking for *his* sister too. He wouldn't want to stay there, he's being forced, I'm sure. Can you help me…please?' A voice deep inside Tara told her this woman could help so she pleaded as earnestly as she could.

'I am sure your friend will come to no real harm with Sylvia. We spirits of the trees get lonely sometimes, just as humans do. She is good at heart and never roams far from her home.'

Tara shuddered. 'Well she charmed my friend, so she can't be that good. Our younger sisters are lost and we were looking for them. Now I need to find them…then we can all go back together to Sylvia's tree, to help Jared.'

Hylda's eyes twinkled indulgently at her. 'Well…'

'Please, can you help me find them?' pleaded Tara again as she struggled to control her tears.

Hylda pursed her lips and nodded, her russet eyes glowing with warmth and understanding. 'I have indeed seen two children pass this way and you will find them a short way down the path, they are accompanied by a lone spriggan.'

'A spriggan?'

'Yes, without his troop, rather strange, but do not be too

concerned, spriggans will generally leave you alone as long as you leave them alone.'

'Oh thank...thank you,' cried Tara. She turned to go.

'If your friend is indeed spellbound, do not let him accept food or drink from Sylvia,' said Hylda, 'or he will stay with her forever as her companion.'

'Thank you...thank you, very much' said Tara again, guessing tree spirits stuck together good or bad. So in fact, Hylda was kind to tell her these things.

'Now, make haste, child,' said Hylda. 'Be firm with Sylvia and all will be well.'

Chapter Eight

Spurred on by the thought Niamh and Lucy were close by, Tara ran along the path. At last they could continue on together and look for her sister and father, if it wasn't for Jared that was. If only she and Niamh had come by themselves. This was their adventure. Now, they had to rescue Jared and much as she'd like to, they couldn't just leave him. How scared Niamh and Lucy must be all by themselves, they would be so happy to see her.

Out of breath, she rounded a corner and her heart jumped with joy, until she saw one of the small creatures with the bulbous heads they had encountered earlier. So that was a spriggan. Niamh and Lucy, who weren't acting scared in the least, walked along with him. She shook with relief. But just in case they were bewitched, she kept a little way behind.

Soon it became clear they were all chatting and even laughing. Niamh and Lucy didn't appear to be in any danger at all, she hurried to catch them up.

Hearing her footsteps, Niamh turned. 'Tara!' she yelled and ran towards her. Tara saw a look of despair cross the face of the spriggan as Niamh threw her arms out to give her a big hug. Lucy ran over and joined in.

'I'm so happy to see you,' said Tara. She glanced at the spriggan; he was even uglier than the others she had seen, his face pitted with scars.

Excited, Niamh jumped up and down and gave her another hug. 'You did come through the gateway after all then.'

'Zalen said you couldn't have come through or you would be here,' said Lucy frowning. 'Where's Jared?'

Tara glowered at Zalen the spriggan, but he immediately looked away. 'We can't stop...we...we have to go back for Jared.' Tara suddenly felt responsible for Jared's predicament even though he got himself into it. Or did he? Tara had known there was something not right about Sylvia…about the situation. She should have done more, insisted they go on. Even if she hadn't been able to persuade him, she could have stayed with him when he fell asleep. Sylvia clearly didn't want her there. She would have had to let them go eventually. But then again, say they had both eaten something. Tara didn't know what to think.

'Back? Why, what's happened to him?' squeaked Lucy, her hands covering her mouth as she waited for Tara's answer.

Tara quickly explained. She also told them what Hylda had said about Jared not eating or drinking and that she had seen Sylvia preparing food.

'We have to go back right now!' cried Lucy, her voice rising.

'It is not safe,' said Zalen. 'We must press on to the palace. We will have to go back for the young man later. I doubt he will come to any real harm in the meantime.'

Hylda had said spriggans were all right as long as you didn't bother them, but Tara wasn't so sure. There was something about him. Her instincts crept in again, and she hadn't been wrong about Sylvia. It wasn't just because he was reluctant to go back to help Jared, he'd also told Niamh and Lucy she and Jared hadn't come through the gateway. Nor had she forgotten how big spriggans could grow or how menacing they could look.

'Jared and I saw more small people like him.' She pointed to Zalen. 'Spriggans can suddenly grow massive and horrible. One of them hit Jared!'

The spriggan looked startled and his eyes filled with fear. 'More…like me? Where? Where was this?' He began to dance about hardly knowing which way to turn.

Tara was disconcerted to see the spriggan afraid of his own kind. 'Well, er, it was back at the mound. There were lots of them.'

'We have to go on,' insisted Zalen. 'It really is not safe here.'

'No, we have to go back,' cried Lucy. 'He's my brother.' Her eyes filled with tears.

Tara gave Zalen one of her, *don't mess with me* looks she had picked up from Uncle Fergus. 'We're going back for Jared, and that's all there is to it. It's not that far. You don't have to come.'

'No need to get snotty, Tara,' said Niamh, scowling at her, 'he's only trying to help.'

What was it with everyone they thought these fae folk friendly just because they spoke kindly, thought Tara? Was she the only one who could see through them? Well, she didn't care. Someone had to watch out for the dangers.

'You can come or stay, Zalen, whatever you want to do, but we're going,' snapped Tara, and grabbing Niamh and Lucy by their sleeves began to pull them back up the path.

'This is madness,' groaned Zalen, hobbling after them. Tara was pleased her firmness has won them over – it was good practice for tackling Sylvia.

On the way back to the ancient oak, Niamh told Tara about how they met Zalen, and in turn, she recounted her own adventures. Tara felt comforted Niamh and Lucy hadn't run off together and left her with Jared. Of course they wouldn't do that, she should have realised. It was strange though they had landed all that distance away from the mound. Something wasn't right about that.

Walking along the path through the darker part of the forest didn't hold the same fear as it had when she was on her own.

Niamh and Lucy linked arms and began to speculate excitedly about the palace they would be visiting. Tara didn't like the idea of going to see Princess Gwyn, whoever she was, but she was at a loss to know what else they could do or where they should go next. What she couldn't understand was why Zalen offered to help them? Could it be out of the goodness of his heart? Most likely he was running away from the other spriggans, but that didn't mean he was trying to do them any harm. Surely not everyone in this realm was wicked, she could be wrong about him after all.

She stole a glance at him, his expression was sober and his eyes darted from side to side as if he expected to be attacked at any moment. They would just have to watch him – very closely.

A few minutes later, Tara guessed they must be near to Sylvia's tree as several old oaks edged the path. She stopped and looked around. 'I think we're here.'

Everyone waited in silence as Tara scrutinised the surroundings. There it was – she was sure of it, a large gnarled oak, fly agaric at the base, mistletoe among the branches. 'I think this is the one!' said Tara excitedly, but when she ran over, the scarf wasn't there. She checked around her. No – something was wrong, she decided. This wasn't the right tree at all.

'Wait a minute...' Niamh pointed along the path to a similar tree. 'That oak also has fly agaric mushrooms and mistletoe!'

Tara ran up to it. What was going on?

'Tara, you twit!' shouted Niamh. 'You should have looked more closely.'

'I did! There was only the one oak with mushrooms and mistletoe. Sylvia must have taken the scarf and enchanted these trees so I couldn't find the way back! We'll just have to check them all.'

They moved on checking every oak they could see, but to Tara they looked too similar. Lucy and Niamh began to call Jared's name at every tree. Silly as she felt doing it, she joined in.

With rising anxiety, Tara stopped in front of yet another oak with mushrooms and mistletoe. It didn't look right. There had to be some way to figure this out...she had to think rationally. If this was another charm, maybe the mushrooms weren't real. She bent down and touched one. Her fingers met having passed right through it and the mushroom instantly vanished and in its place was plain old grass.

'Sylvia has used glamour,' said Zalen. 'It is a kind of charm where something appears different than it really is.'

Tara realised that's what had happened when her own clothes

had changed to the white gossamer dress, yet it seemed so convincing. She turned to the others. 'The mushrooms aren't real. If you touch them, they disappear.'

Niamh and Lucy ran over.

'Dryads are tricky creatures,' said Zalen somewhat admiringly.

That would go for pretty much everyone they had met so far in the Otherworld, thought Tara. She stared back down the path and Niamh eyes followed her direction.

'We have to go back and check the ones we've already passed,' said Niamh, in an exasperated voice.

Lucy groaned. 'How do we do that?'

'We need to touch a mushroom at each tree to see if they're fake or not. If they're not fake, they'll be solid, which means it's the right tree...okay?'

'We had better get started!' said Zalen with urgency. 'We cannot hang around long, especially if you want to stop your friend from eating.'

Tara glared incredulously at him, that wasn't what he was saying earlier when he wanted to leave Jared behind. But there was no time to stand and wonder about it. She ran back to the previous oak and was just about to check the mushrooms there when out of the trees trotted the white stag. He bowed his great head at them and trotted off down the path stopping at one of the oaks. He began to act skittish, jumping around.

'That must be the right tree!' said Tara. 'That's what he's telling us!'

She didn't wait to explain herself, but sprinted back to the tree. The stag backed off and walked away. As Niamh and Lucy arrived by her side, two collared doves flew out of the branches, their wings flapping noisily. Tara stroked a mushroom – it was solid. The tree suddenly appeared so much bigger than the others. Glamour, they would have to watch out for that.

'How do we get inside?' asked Lucy.

'Sylvia touched the tree like this.' Tara put two hands on the tree, the cold bark rough beneath her fingers. Nothing happened. 'A door should appear. At first it's a bit fuzzy, and when it becomes clear you can walk through it.'

Lucy put her hands on the tree. Still nothing happened.

'Let Niamh try,' suggested Zalen. 'She is a child of this realm and must hold some magical power.'

Niamh grimaced and shrugging her shoulders put her hands on the trunk. No doorway appeared, not even a glimmer of one.

'Concentrate!' cried Tara. 'You have to fight her magic!'

'I am!' retorted Niamh.

At last an outline appeared. Niamh took heart and her face screwed up with the effort as if she was trying to push the tree down. Increasingly, the doorway became more transparent and Tara ran to Niamh's side to look through it. They could see two figures inside. Jared was awake and sitting in one of the chairs, his eyes wide and unblinking as if in a trance. Sylvia was approaching him with a tray of food.

Lucy squeezed between them and banged her fists on the doorway.

'Don't Lucy...she might see us!' snapped Tara.

It was too late. Sylvia turned and looked hard at them, but Jared didn't move...didn't hear.

Sylvia set the tray down on a small side table, and took a piece of bread from it. She smiled, and handed it to Jared.

'Jared! Jared! Listen to us, don't eat!' yelled Lucy.

Jared took the bread.

'We're coming!' shrieked Niamh.

Tara put her own hands on the doorway and concentrated hard. Suddenly she was in mid-air before falling hard on the floor. Niamh fell with her.

In a flash, Lucy jumped over them and ran to Jared, snatching the bread from his hand, but was just too late, as he had already taken a bite. Lucy thumped him heartily on the back. 'Spit it out,

Jared.'

'Yes, spit it out,' called Niamh. Luckily, Jared did as he was told and spat it out.

Sylvia stepped back, an expression of mock surprise on her face. Niamh and Tara picked themselves up and rushed over to Jared.

He stared ahead, not seeing them. Lucy took hold of his hands. 'Jared! Jared!' she called softly. 'Jared, it's me!' But he didn't move.

'Let me try,' demanded Niamh, pushing her way in. 'Wake up, Jared.' Her voice was loud and firm.

Jared's expression gradually softened, and he rapidly blinked several times. Rubbing his eyes, he finally realised who stood in front of him. Tara breathed a sigh of relief.

'Niamh...Lucy...how did *you* get here?' he gasped. 'W-what happened?'

'Sylvia bewitched you!' exclaimed Lucy scowling at Sylvia who was standing with her back to the food table. 'She tried to keep you here with her!'

'What nonsense,' said Sylvia. 'You were clearly tired and I was only being hospitable. Your friends are a little over anxious, I think.'

'No we're not. If he'd eaten the bread he *would* have to stay with you...forever!' Tara persisted.

Jared gaped at her as if she were the mad one. Oh, how exasperating he was, and after she had saved him from becoming some sort of slave. Well if that's all the gratitude she got...

'I meant you no harm,' said Sylvia pouting.

'Oh yes you did,' rasped Tara. She turned back to Jared. 'We just stopped you from eating the bread in time.'

Jared frowned and shook his head in disbelief. 'Hey, what are you all talking about? She just wanted to help us. And I only swallowed a few crumbs.'

'A few crumbs!' groaned Tara, wondering what it would now

mean. 'She was trying to keep you here. You *have* to believe us!'

Lucy threw her arms around him. 'Never mind, at least you're safe now.'

'Geroff Luce!' Jared struggled unsteadily to his feet.

Sylvia moved to the doorway. Zalen was nowhere to be seen. 'Out of our way,' demanded Tara. This time there would be no keeping anyone captive.

Sylvia stood her ground. Her expression went from one of defiance to one of contriteness. 'I was made to do it,' she said. 'I was scared not to.'

'Who made you do it then?' asked Tara, not believing her. Still this time, she had to admit to herself, Sylvia appeared to be telling the truth.

Sylvia's face lost all fight. It was as if a veil had fallen from it. She looked vulnerable and afraid. 'I cannot say, or she will surely kill me,' she whimpered. 'I am sorry, you have to believe me. I will make amends to you, Jared. I will – I promise!'

'What you did was wrong!' said Tara sharply, wishing she could punish her for bewitching Jared, but her resolve weakened at the misery on Sylvia's face. Unexpectedly, she was no longer afraid of Sylvia or her enchantments. Tara instinctively knew she had lost her power over them. 'We don't need anything from you. Now move out of the way.' She kept her voice firm, remembering Hylda's words.

Sylvia reluctantly moved away from the doorway.

'What sort of amends?' asked Jared.

'You will see.'

Tara glowered at her. 'We don't need your kind of help.' She grabbed Jared's arm and snatched his coat and Niamh's scarf from the chair. 'Come on. Let's get as far away from here as possible.' They all stumbled out through the open door, which closed behind them. Tara was relieved Jared could leave the tree, which surely meant the few crumbs he swallowed hadn't affected him. Finally, they could continue with what they came here to do.

The sooner they got away from this area the better.

Zalen reappeared. Tara glared at him. What had he been doing during their time in the tree, she questioned, and why hadn't he shown himself? He was definitely hiding, and not just from the spriggans.

'You fancied her, Jared,' sniggered Lucy, interrupting her train of thought.

'No I didn't.' He gave Lucy a shove.

Lucy shoved him back.

'Stop it, you two,' snapped Tara. 'You're acting like five-year-olds. We need to get out of here.' She marched on ahead of them. Jared was just so childish. She wished they'd left him behind with Sylvia; she could have fattened him up and eaten him for all she cared.

Niamh and Zalen caught up with her. Niamh tucked her arm into her own and Tara instantly felt better. They were all together, all safe, and that's all that mattered. Tara decided they must find help. At home it all seemed so easy, a possible adventure. So far it was more like a nightmare, she wished she could just wake up and find herself back home, safe in her bed.

As soon as they travelled far enough from the tree to be out of danger, Tara suggested they stop and eat something. Her tummy growled like mad. Better to eat their own food than have Jared tempted to eat anything he saw.

'Good idea, then maybe it will stop Jared from accepting food from pretty strangers,' joked Lucy from behind them echoing her own thoughts.

Finding a spot where the sun came through the trees, they sat on a fallen tree trunk.

'We'll have to be careful with the food,' stated Tara, 'now that we only have one backpack and it has to go around the four of us.' It was warmer now – she took off her scarf and laid it on the ground.

'Five of us,' said Zalen.

Tara was about to remark on it, before deciding it would be petty. They each took a squashed cheese sandwich.

'What's the place called we're going to?' asked Jared, reaching for another sandwich the second he swallowed the last mouthful of his first one.

Tara slapped his hand away from the food. 'It's a palace.'

'Yes Vrogoly Palace, and we need to go now,' said Zalen, swallowing a sandwich in one go. 'We've delayed long enough and we still have a river to cross.' He stood up and began to walk towards the path.

They all gathered up their belongings. Tara handed Niamh her scarf and wrapped her own back around her neck. Niamh put her arm through Lucy's and seeing Jared hurrying over to speak, Tara ran a few steps to Niamh's other side. She wasn't in the mood for him right now, neither did she want to discuss Sylvia and she had a feeling he did. Not that she was interested in Lucy's babyish chatter about princesses and palaces either. Anyway, from what she had experienced so far, she didn't have much hope the palace was as grand, safe and filled with precious jewels and princes as Lucy seemed to think. Though secretly she wished it was exactly like that.

They had been walking for a while and had long left behind the area where she had finally found Niamh and Lucy. Zalen had quickened the pace, though still paid attention to the surroundings, being aware of anything and everything. This time Tara realised he was searching for something. She hoped it meant the palace wasn't so far away.

A few minutes later Zalen wandered into the trees. He turned to them. 'Here we are at last, a hidden pathway.'

'What pathway?' asked Jared, nonplussed.

Tara went into the trees to where Zalen stood. There was no pathway.

'*Look*,' said Zalen. 'You need to *look*. It is there.'

They all stood now searching ahead of them.

'Hey!' yelled Niamh. 'I can see it. Let your eyes go a bit out of focus.'

It took a minute or so, but sure enough, Tara could see a narrow path winding in and out of the trees.

'Do not worry,' said Zalen to Jared and Lucy, 'Once you are on it you will be able to see it too.'

They trekked in single file, as the path was narrow. Zalen led the way while Jared lagged at the back. Ahead of them, a wren warbled a song while a jay screeched as it flew between the trees. Tara felt safer off the main pathway. Zalen had said this was a hidden path, but how many people knew the secret of it? Not many she hoped.

'Hello!' said Jared out of the blue, causing everyone to turn around. He was staring at a spot under a birch tree, but Tara could see there was no one there.

Chapter Nine

Donella looked out of the window. How she hated it here at Caer Searesby. Why she could not stay with Aunt Gwyn all the time, she did not know. As it was, she was lucky to see her a few times a year.

Two days ago, just when she had been so looking forward to her annual overnight birthday visit to Vrogoly palace, which coincided with her betrothal, her Aunt Marvaanagh had told her she must not venture from the west wing. So, she had spent her sixteenth birthday unpacking, and apart from a short period of fresh air and exercise in the inner ward, she had not left her room or seen anyone except for her aunt's servant Zalen, then again it was better than seeing no one at all.

Donella was looking forward to her forthcoming marriage to Mawgan, Prince of Dumnonia. For then she would have more freedom as she would finally become Queen of the Realm of Wiltunscire, and could do as she pleased. Oh, there would be so many changes. Somehow though, she had a feeling her aunt would not be happy with them.

Later today she had something to look forward to, Mawgan and his uncle, King Branwalather, would arrive for the formal betrothal. The papers would be brought here to Caer Searesby to be signed by her Aunt Marvaanagh before being taken to her Aunt Gwyn. Donella was under no illusion as to why Aunt Marvaanagh and King Branwalather had arranged the betrothal...they both wanted some control over the Realm of Wiltunscire through her. Aunt Gwyn had told her so.

If only her parents were here safe with her in Wiltunscire, there would be no marriage, there would be no power battles, and her life would be very different. Oh why had her parents taken her to the Realm of Glastenning that day many years ago? Now they were trapped on the secret island Ynys Is. And like all the folk who became trapped there, they were good as dead, frozen in time, never to return. As much as Donella hated it, if it were not for her Aunt Marvaanagh, she would be with her parents, frozen forever, and her aunt reminded her of that fact daily.

Donella had three legal guardians, her mother's younger sister, Queen Marvaanagh; her elder brother, King Branwalather; and her father's aunt, Princess Gwyn. Marvaanagh had insisted on bringing her up. King Branwalather's wife had died many years before and his kingdom suffered regular raids from the Kawpangian tribes, and Princess Gwyn was elderly, so there could be no argument.

How Donella loved her Aunt Gwyn. If only she had been younger and in better health, Donella could have lived at Vrogoly Palace and been so much happier. But Mawgan was on his way. Donella hoped he remained the same sweet man she had always found him to be. It was a few months since she had seen him last on one of the rare state visits. Mawgan and Donella had a brief chance to walk together in the grounds. They realised they liked each other and got on very well. At least that was something, she decided. Marriage to him would be tolerable. Anyway, who else would she marry?

One of their favourite games when they were children was to play hide-and-seek all over the castle. That was when Mawgan had showed her the secret passageway from the long gallery down to the buttery, where the wine was kept. His uncle had told him few people knew of it, including Marvaanagh. They would sneak down and through to the kitchens and take food out of the larder for midnight snacks. In fact, that was exactly what she would do now. Hunger pangs gnawed at her stomach and at least she would get out of the west wing for a while.

Donella tiptoed from her room, quietly closed the door behind her, and crept along the hallway. At the far end of the gallery was a carved panel, which if pressed in a particular way, would open and reveal the passageway. It was dark in there though, she would need a light. At the end of the hallway was a store cupboard; she knew she would find a tinderbox there. Hurrying to it, she pulled it open and was pleased to find one next to a box of candles; she slipped it into her pocket before proceeding into the gallery.

The long gallery was one of her favourite places. On rainy days, she liked to wander up and down looking at the beautifully carved oak panels, the many paintings of her ancestors, which adorned the walls, and the colourful tapestries that hung in between. On one side of the gallery, the many west-facing windows provided her with wonderful views of the surrounding land…her land. She often came to sit in a window seat and watch the world go by, or later in the day, the glowing sunset.

Here and there, oil lamps were set into nooks in the wall, and going to the one nearest to her, Donella struck the flint a few times causing the small piece of cloth in the tinderbox to ignite. She lit the lamp, and blew out the flames in the tinderbox.

Further along the gallery, she found a wooden panel beautifully carved with roses. She searched quickly for one particular rose. Finding it, she pressed the centre and the panel clicked open. Glancing around to check no one was watching, and seeing it was all clear, she slipped through the gap, closing the panel behind her. She left the tinderbox on the floor and moved swiftly down the twisting stone steps.

At the bottom, a narrow dark corridor lay in front of her. In the depth of the castle, it was cold and smelt dank, but worse, it was airless and suffocating. Taking a breath, she hurried along, having no wish to meet any spiders or rats that might be lurking there.

At last, she came to the doorway. Leaving the lamp on the floor, she clicked open the latch. The passageway came out behind a wine rack. Hearing no one on the other side, she pushed it open. A slight grating echoed round the room, but luckily, no one was in sight. She slid the rack back into place and continued up the stairs to the hallway leading to the kitchens.

Halfway along, Donella passed an open window. Her Aunt Marvaanagh stood outside talking to the captain of her new guard, one of the grislic goblins. She quickly ducked and sat under the window, waiting.

Her aunt's voice drifted through. 'Send a message to Grud and Dargen by carrier falcon. Inform them they must go to Vrogoly Forest immediately to find those accursed children before they reach the palace. Bring them here to the dungeon. There are four. They travel together with the spriggan called Zalen. If they have to slay the three human children in the taking, then no matter, but the other they must take alive. They will know her. She is a child of the realms, with long, dark hair very similar to my own. She will be wearing a bracelet of gold, which has a precious stone the colour of her eyes, indigo. It protects her and cannot be removed.' Her aunt's voice was tight and controlled and a wave of nausea engulfed Donella as she continued, '…As for the traitor Zalen, tell them they must kill him on sight!'

Donella gasped, how despicable, kill children, kill Zalen! This was her own aunt talking, how could she be so wicked.

Donella thought of her own treatment over the years, the lack of love, the fake concern for her, her virtual imprisonment, she should not be surprised. But if she tried telling anyone, no one would believe her. Her Aunt Marvaanagh, once hated in the Realm of Wiltunscire had won the respect of the people by caring for the darling of the realm, the poor orphaned child Donella. Donella knew better though, as her Aunt Gwyn had told her that in Marvaanagh's own realm of Glastenning, especially the Isle of Avallach, where her castle was situated, her people feared and hated her.

Much of Glastenning was made up of small islands, including the fearful and secret Ynys Is where her parents had become trapped and which could only be accessed by a map, and who had the map no one knew as it has been stolen from the spriggans of Dumnonia who were the usual custodians of it.

The talking had ceased, so Donella crawled from her place under the window and jumping to her feet, lifted her long skirts and ran back along the corridor to the buttery. She slipped through the door of the passageway, and grabbing the lamp ran back up the stairway. Remembering to extinguish the lamp, she left it inside the doorway next to the tinderbox, that way if she wanted to use the passageway again she would have less chance of anyone seeing her if she did not have to go searching for a lamp and something to light it with first.

Back in her room, she lay on her bed thinking. What could she do to warn those children…those human children? She had never met a human before. She wondered what they looked like, and why her aunt wanted the dark-haired realm girl so much. Mostly though, she was curious as to why the girl had a bracelet the same as her own.

She held up her wrist. The bracelet was passed to the heir, whether boy or girl. Once it had been her mother's and now it was hers. The stone in it took on the colour of the wearer's eyes, and for her, the stone was indigo. It protected the prince or princess of Wiltunscire until they had a child themselves, then at a time deemed suitable, it would be passed on to him or her.

So this girl, the wearer of the bracelet, must be at the very least of royal blood. Most likely, she belonged to one of the outer realms; she must try to warn her and the human children…but how? There was no one in the castle she could trust. She had no friends only Mawgan, yes Mawgan, he would help her and what was more, he would be travelling to Vrogoly Palace on the morrow. He would help, she was sure of it.

Chapter Ten

'Pleased to meet you too...Leanne,' Jared said to the empty spot. He patted the air.

Lucy was nearest to him, 'Er...who are you talking to, Jared?'

'To the little girl, of course.'

Tara moved closer, scanning the undergrowth for the little girl. 'Where is she then?'

'She's right in front of you, noodle. Open your eyes!'

'I'm not a noodle,' snapped Tara. 'We haven't time for your stupid jokes.'

'It's not a joke! You're the one who's joking. You must be able to see her!'

Niamh laughed. 'There's no one there, Jared.'

Lucy put her hand on his forehead. 'Are you all right, Jared?'

Jared scowled at them. 'Don't be stupid, you lot.'

'We're not the ones who are joking,' said Tara seriously. She could really do without his silly games. If he wanted to act like an idiot, she would treat him like one. 'You're the one who has the imaginary friend.'

'She's not imaginary! She's a little kid, about seven years old, with yellow hair. She even told me her name...Leanne! You must be able to see her!'

'Obviously not. I think we'd better go on,' said Tara, not bothering to hide the sneer in her voice. 'You can bring your friend with you if you want.'

Niamh and Lucy sniggered.

'Urghhhh! She *is* there. It's not my fault you can't see her!'

He turned back to the tree. 'Let them see you, will you,' he urged. 'They think I'm nuts.' He stood for a second frowning before looking up again. 'She says she can't. She's only attached to me.'

'It is probably because he ate the breadcrumbs,' said Zalen. 'I do not know how long the charm will last, could be forever. The child could be imaginary or real.'

'That's just great,' groaned Tara. She walked on, looking back to see Jared half-turning and holding out his hand.

'Okay, you can come with us,' she heard him say.

Tara was tired; they'd been travelling for some time along the secret pathway without any rest. The forest had now become very dense and dark. The path was difficult to navigate. They had to watch every step, as rocks and tree roots littered their way, and every so often they came across a steep incline or decline, which they had to slip and slide up or down.

An eerie rustling sounded to both sides of them and imperceptible movements in the grey shadows convinced Tara someone was watching them. How much further could it be to the river...and what was that awful stench?

There was a gasp behind her.

Before Tara had time to turn, somebody grabbed at her leg. She screamed and Niamh shrieked right into her ear. Tara jumped with the pain of it.

Two creatures leapt about eventually landing on the path. Their hideous appearance sickened Tara, she screamed again. Small, about knee high, with stubby ears, mean eyes, and pointed noses far too huge for their repugnant faces, they blocked the way. They stank and the one that kept grabbing at her leg grinned revealing a set of yellow, crooked teeth. Hair sprouted out from every bit of exposed skin, especially on his forehead, his clothes were dark and ragged, and a dirty hat covering his head, hadn't seen soap and water for many years.

'Get away!' screeched Tara, kicking out trying to shake him off.

Jared pushed forward and booted it, sending it flying into the bracken. He charged after the other one, which immediately began to back off.

'No need for that, young human.' croaked the creature. 'We grislic goblins are *friendly* folk.' He bowed, taking off his hat and sweeping it in front of him in a mock grand, but horribly grotesque gesture, he said, 'Grud at your service. '

The other creature scrambled out of the bracken and skulked forward, staring malevolently at Jared before bowing to Niamh alone.

'...and this is Dargen.'

'Out of our way!' ordered Jared.

Tara turned to see why Zalen hadn't come forward, but he'd gone again. 'We're in a hurry so please get out of our way,' she said.'

'In a hurry to where, I wonder,' joined in the creature called Grud.

'To Vrogoly Palace,' piped up Lucy. They all turned and glared at her.

'Out of our way, we said!' roared Jared.

Without warning, Grud and Dargen leapt on Jared knocking him off his feet.

Leaping over him, they turned their attention to Niamh. Grabbing her, they began dragging her into the trees. Niamh screamed and struggled, while Lucy pulled at her coat trying to hang onto her.

Tara picked up a stick not knowing quite what she intended. Where was the stag, why didn't he come to their rescue? Looking around it struck her the forest was too dense for such a big stag, he wasn't going to come.

Jared, back on his feet, tore the stick from her hand and went after the goblins. He wacked Grud who looked at him so venomously that Jared jumped back. Tara screeched as Grud's hand shot out and his long nails scraped down Jared's face. Jared fell back out of the way almost as if he'd been pushed by an invisible hand, otherwise Grud would have clawed him again.

The goblins continued to drag Niamh into the undergrowth

with Lucy in tow, still hanging onto Niamh's coat. 'Let her go!' she cried.

Tara picked up the stick Jared had dropped and rained blows on Grud's arm.

Jared leapt back on his feet, found another stick and joined her. 'Yes, let her go!'

Grud let go of Niamh and grasping both sticks, yanked them roughly out of their hands. Once again he grabbed Niamh. Suddenly, a huge rock flew through the air and hit the ground close to Grud. Another followed it and more in quick succession, one landing on Dargen's foot. He yelled out in pain and hopped around. Another hit Grud on the shoulder and at last he let Niamh go.

Someone was helping them. 'Run,' screamed Tara, and all four of them ran back onto the path, as more rocks rained down on the goblins, who quickly vanished into the undergrowth.

From behind a big oak, a full-size male spriggan stepped. Danger again, Tara immediately thought, but the scars on his face identified him as Zalen. He shrank back to his normal size and fell over.

'That hurts,' he whimpered.

Jared ran over to him and helped him up. Niamh and Lucy went over and patted his back, Tara joined them.

Zalen cleared his throat and coughed. 'Come on, we are nearly at the river, we need to reach the palace before nightfall. He turned and led the way.

Jared walked beside Tara. 'Leanne saved me you know,' he whispered to her.

'What do you mean, Leanne saved you. She's not real, you've been charmed.'

'She is real and she pushed me out of the way of Grud's nails, otherwise I'd be as scarred as Zalen and not just have a scratch.'

'I doubt it,' said Tara.

'Doubt what? That I'd be scarred or that Leanne saved me?'

'Both,' said Tara. Still, she has seen Jared thrown back by something. But he was charmed, which probably had something to do with it.

Over the next few minutes it became gloomier, as a strong breeze got up blowing a dark and ominous cloud their way. The trees began to sway, whistling louder and louder. The atmosphere had turned a sickly yellow and a heavy drop of rain landed on Tara's cheek.

Jared, Lucy, and Niamh, pulled up their hoods. Tara didn't have one, and hoped it would just be a shower. It wasn't. Lightning flashed across the sky.

'There is something wrong,' muttered Zalen, scratching his head. 'The sky was clear blue a moment ago. The weather does not change this quickly. Come we need to hurry to the bridge.'

Soon the drops turned into a heavy downpour, the rain lashed horizontally, as thunder roared above them.

Lucy struggled against the wind, now more like a gale, so Tara took her arm. Together they battled against the full force of the driving rain that came down so hard it hurt.

They all stopped briefly under a tree, the raindrops pounded heavily and noisily through the branches as they huddled together. The trees howled a protest and another great streak of lightning flashed across the sky. Eyes sought eyes, but no one spoke. It wasn't safe.

They moved away from the lone tree just as an ear-splitting clap of thunder crashed above them, followed not long after by a bright light, a bang and the smell of burning. The tree was struck in two and another clap of thunder scared Tara out of her wits. Lucy screamed and put one hand over her head to protect it from falling branches and twigs, clinging to Tara with the other.

They hurried away. It was difficult to walk, not just because of the might of the rain, and the sudden strong gusts of wind, but because the water now sloshed around their feet, which sank into the sodden ground.

At last they came upon the river. They still had a little way to go to reach the bridge, which Tara could see in the distance.

The muddy river was gathering energy, gushing wild and furious, surging and rising higher by the second. The waterfowl flew off with a noisy flapping of wings, quacking and honking. Battling on, the rain fell harder and harder, it was as if someone was pouring water from a great urn in the sky right down on them.

After what seemed an age, Tara looked up to see quite a way ahead, Niamh hanging onto Jared's coat, Zalen hard at their heels. They had reached the bridge. Zalen turned and shouted something, but his words were lost on the wind. They carried on across the bridge.

'We need to hurry, I think,' Tara shouted to Lucy.

Finally, heads down, they stepped onto the bridge themselves, which was built from wood, and every step was an effort as they walked across.

Halfway, Tara looked up to see how far ahead the others had got, when an horrendous noise like a train crashing, caused her to reel back and grasp the handrail.

With great effort and filled with trepidation, she turned around to see a massive wave surging towards them, carrying with it all manner of debris. It was going to hit the bridge.

The others, now safely at the other side, had jumped onto the bank and were screaming words she couldn't hear, but could guess at.

Feeling the movement of the wooden structure beneath them, Tara reached out gripping Lucy tightly. The bridge began to creak and groan followed by a loud cracking noise as it gave way.

The full power of the freezing water crashed into them, knocking them off their feet, snatching Tara's breath away. She managed to hook one arm around the handrail, trying her best to hold onto Lucy with the other. As one side of the bridge collapsed, Lucy's feet scrabbled to keep a footing, but she slipped down the wooden planks. Tara lost her grip, but managed to grab Lucy's hand as she held it out. She was left dangling over the water.

'I can't hold on, Tara. Don't let me fall! Please don't let go!' Lucy begged, her hand beginning to slip from Tara's.

There was no time to think. 'No, I won't let you go, Lucy.' With that, Tara let go of the handrail and they plunged together into the raging torrent.

As they fell, Tara made a grab for Lucy. They sank under the water for a few seconds. When they emerged gasping and spluttering, Tara managed to get behind Lucy and grasp her under the arms. Lucy struggled making it difficult for Tara to keep hold.

The floodwater carried them away. Branches and logs rushed by. Tara's instincts were to throw out her arms to fight the current, but she was conscious that doing so would mean letting go of Lucy.

Tara was on her back and her own head kept going under the water. Strangely, she wasn't frightened nor was she gasping for air. It was just like at home in the bath, but this time the water didn't rise, yet she could stay under without problem.

They tumbled on down the river. Tara had to use every bit of her strength to keep Lucy's head above the water. Keeping calm she knew was the most important thing. She let the water take them where it wanted. The riverbank wasn't so far away, if only she could somehow steer them towards it, but the river was still too strong and it was difficult avoiding all the debris. A large log came towards them and she just managed to pull Lucy out of its way.

Tara began to grow weary. She had always been a strong swimmer, but never had to face anything like this. Every time they twisted around so Tara could see what was ahead, she searched for a way to get to the riverbank.

Suddenly, there was Niamh running along the path shouting and holding out her hands.

In front of Niamh, the water had calmed, but it was close to the bank and they were still caught in the main torrent. Tara attempted to manoeuvre them towards it, but couldn't make it.

Niamh held out her hands again and the water became less furious about them. At least Lucy didn't thrash about so much now, as Tara was so tired trying to keep hold of her. Horrified, she realised why Lucy wasn't struggling...she was unconscious.

Tara put her hand out in another attempt to swim to the bank. She gasped in astonishment. Her fingers were joined together, webbed like her toes. Now she knew she must be losing consciousness too, she was hallucinating. It had happened once before when she was small and had a fever. She'd imagined bees swarming all over her and it was horrible.

She looked across to the bank in panic, and glimpsed something in the water...the white stag. She hoped and prayed he was real and not part of her hallucination. He swam towards them.

With renewed strength, Tara did her best to keep Lucy above water. Eventually the stag came alongside them. Without hesitation, she grabbed his antlers with one hand, and he pulled them towards the bank.

...Something was trying to tug Lucy from her arms. She tried to hold on until she saw people in the water helping them and she gratefully let go of both Lucy and the stag's antlers.

Hands pulled Tara from the water onto the bank. More people stood around her, small like the spriggans and goblins, this time they had pleasant round faces. The clouds and rain had dwindled away and the sky was clear again.

Tara collapsed to her knees on the grass. She looked down at her hands, but there was no sign of the webbing. Phew, she had imagined it after all.

It didn't seem long before Niamh was by her side.

'Lucy...?'

'Lucy's fine,' said Niamh. 'She's awake again...just a bit cold.'

Tara could see a group of the small people gathered around a small form, which she realised must be Lucy. They were chafing her hands. The stag was nowhere in sight.

Zalen came over when he saw her staring. 'It is all right, they are brownies.'

Two of the brownies came over and began to rub Tara's hands.

'I am Guido and this is Udell,' said the brownie, in a surprisingly deep voice for such a tiny person. He was older than the other brownie and had side-whiskers.

'Are you headed for Vrogoly Palace?'

'Yes, we are,' replied Niamh.

'Do you think you could get up?' Udell asked Tara, his voice high pitched, almost a squeak. 'It is dusk and soon it will be dark. We need to be on our way.'

Tara shivered now with the cold, but was unhurt apart from a few scratches. 'Yes, I think so.'

They helped her to her feet.

'We should carry the little one,' Guido said to Udell.

'I will do it,' offered Zalen, with that, he immediately began to grow to full height. He picked Lucy up, much to the surprise of Tara, who was feeling a bit guilty for not trusting him. Tara knew it caused him some effort to grow.

Jared came over and offered Tara his arm. She was too tired to protest so she took it. Niamh came to her other side and they set off back into the forest.

'I wasn't going to tell you this, as I'm sure no one will believe me,' said Niamh. 'I prayed for the water to become calm. And it did. I don't know how I did it, Tara, but honestly it was me...I calmed the water. I just couldn't make it stretch all the way across to you.'

'Don't be daft,' sneered Jared. 'You can't control water, no one can.'

'I'm not surprised at anything that happens anymore,' replied Tara. 'Remember, you have an invisible friend, Jared.' *And I can breathe underwater*, she added to herself,

Tara's legs felt like lead as she struggled to walk on. The river had taken more out of her than she first thought. But yes she breathed under water, that much she hadn't imagined. If Niamh was a child of this land, she wasn't surprised she had some magical ability like most of the other fae folk they'd met. But to have it herself was something she didn't understand. Why? She wasn't a child of these realms. Perhaps she was making more of it than was necessary, after all, she had no other powers, so far anyway, just the breathing underwater...and well yes, the webbed fingers if that was real. There was so much she needed to know, she just hoped someone could answer all their questions.

A few minutes later, Tara gasped in astonishment as the forest dissolved before her eyes, and the path widened into a huge clearing. A magnificent white palace materialised in front of them.

'Ahh,' breathed Niamh.

'Wow!' said Jared.

The palace was huge, a rectangle with four tall turrets and scores of windows. In front of it stretched a delightful landscaped garden with a lawn and small lake. The whole place was lit up with thousands of fireflies hovering or darting about.

'Allow us to show you safe passage.' Guido bowed and turning led the way.

Chapter Eleven

Donella had spent the morning polishing her wavy, black hair with a silk cloth and at last managed to achieve a shine. Her hair never looked right and did not suit her pale complexion. A servant girl came and piled it on top of her head, threading it through with small flowers. Donella hoped it would take the emphasis off her rather unremarkable face. The only thing she liked about herself was her height and slim build.

She twirled around in the white gown her Aunt Marvaanagh had given her to wear; elegant and covered in tiny seed pearls, it glistened with silver thread. She was quite pleased with the whole effect once finished. But would Mawgan even notice?

The ceremony was long and boring. Someone brought a bunch of scrolls into the great hall. Tied around with a blue ribbon, they lay on a blue velvet cushion. No one spoke except the legal people. Donella did not like being on show and was pleased few people stood about the room.

She sat formally on one throne while Mawgan sat on another next to her. A warm feeling came over her when she looked at him. Dressed handsomely in royal blue garments, he had a comforting warmth in his nut brown eyes. Golden threads glinted in his chestnut hair that she had not noticed before, and Donella suddenly felt shy.

The legal men approached and unrolled the scrolls on a table, behind which their aunt and uncle stood. It was they – not Donella or Mawgan – who signed them. Her Aunt Marvaanagh sealed them with the royal seal. Marvaanagh had told Donella she and Mawgan would sign on the day of the marriage. This was set for one week hence. It would be a quiet affair.

Marvaanagh embraced Donella, kissing her on both cheeks. She was dressed in gold, and wore the crown of Glastenning. Her enormous, silk, brocade dress got in the way and Donella stifled a giggle as Marvaanagh struggled to reach her cheek. Her Uncle Branwalather strolled over, embraced her and kissed her. Marvaanagh did the same with Mawgan. Donella did not miss that Mawgan leaned back as she moved towards him. At that point, she warmed to him even more.

Donella did not know what to make of her Uncle Branwalather; she had never had much contact with him before. He was a big man, dressed totally in black with the gold crown of Dumnonia upon his head, the face beneath it lined. Snow-white hair aged him, and his ice-blue eyes did not give away anything of his personality.

Mawgan had told Donella he looked older than he was because of the troubles in Dumnonia these last fifteen years caused by the constant raids by the Kawpangian tribe to unseat him from his throne. Mawgan was related to the king by marriage. He was the nephew of Branwalather's wife, the Queen of Dumnonia, who had been killed in a raid. But they were like father and son, as Mawgan had lost his own parents in the same raid.

'Congratulations, my dear,' Branwalather said, his hands still on her shoulders, his voice sounding as if it had travelled through a gravel pit. 'Welcome to the family branch of Dumnonia.'

'We are not married yet,' retorted Donella.

She recoiled as fire sprang into the ice-blue eyes. 'Ha, you have spirit. You will need it in the coming months.'

There followed a small celebratory feast, which was noticeable for its lack of guests. Apart from herself, Mawgan and her aunt and uncle, there were two small legal men with long beards and her aunt's new personal assistant, a duergar called Braedon. Donella found him creepy, and much preferred Zalen. What had he done to incur such wrath from Marvaanagh? It had something to do with the children Marvaanagh had sent the grislic goblins to find.

The grislic goblins were effective guards as they were the most gruesome and ignorant goblin race of all and Donella was afraid of them. She feared for those children and hoped she would get a chance to speak with Mawgan. In the morning, he and his uncle would leave for Vrogoly Palace, as Aunt Gwyn needed to sign the betrothal scroll. Donella hated it she would not be going.

Mawgan caught her eye. 'It is a little warm in here, would you care for a stroll in the garden before we retire,' he asked.

Marvaanagh's head swept around to them. 'You may n—'

'Good idea. Run along the two of you,' interrupted Branwalather.

Run along, they were to be married next week and he was treating them like small children. Donella decided not complain though as her aunt clearly did not want them to go out. She stepped away from the table and Mawgan came to her side, offering her his arm. A servant brought their cloaks and helped them on with them and they strolled out into the inner ward.

It was strange to Donella that here she was betrothed to a young man she had known for most of her life. It pleased her that he had not changed much since they were children. She was right; marriage to him would be good, and certainly preferable to living with her aunt for another two years. How handsome he was, she was surprised she had not noticed it years ago. He caught her looking and smiled at her, and she felt the warmth rush to her cheeks.

'A strange state of affairs,' said Mawgan as they reached the great fountain. 'What is the rush? We were not supposed to marry for two more years. Something must be stirring in the political pot.'

'Indeed,' agreed Donella. 'But I cannot help wondering if it is somehow connected with the human children and the realm girl.'

'Human children?' Looking back towards the windows of the great hall, Mawgan directed her behind the fountain, out of sight.

Concealed now, Donella was unsure how much she should tell him, but then she did not know much.

'My aunt has called for her servant Zalen to be slain on sight. It has something to do with four children, three of them human, though it appears only the realm child is important. A dark haired girl...my aunt said...wearing a bracelet similar to my own, which is most curious. She must be kept alive, but the other children are dispensable by all accounts.'

'Really...children! Are you sure?'

'I heard my aunt giving the orders myself. Do you remember the secret passageway you showed me? Well I had sneaked down into the kitchens and that is when I overheard her.'

'I am most shocked. I do not particularly like the queen, but I did not think she was capable of such evil. Who are these children?'

'I do not know, just that they are four in number and one is of the realm. My aunt is evil...you have to believe me, she is a cold person, as cold as Ynys Is. The children are somewhere in Vrogoly Forest and as you are to pass that way—'

'Ahh, I see. Well if I see such children I will warn them, do not worry. If it is any consolation, I do believe you. I would hardly think you would make up such a thing. There is something going on and we are both being kept in the dark about it. I intend to find out exactly what it is.'

'Thank you, Mawgan, I knew you would help. If you do not see them could you please find time to tell Aunt Gwyn?'

'You are a good and kind person, Donella.' Mawgan nodded and bending down checked no one was in sight, then kissed her on the cheek causing little butterflies to flutter in her stomach. 'Had any midnight feasts recently?' he asked. 'How about one later?'

Donella laughed feeling much more at ease, as if a heavy

burden was lifting from her.

* * *

Scarlet roses still in colourful bloom lined the path to the grand entrance of the palace and they meandered through a mist of gorgeous fragrance. Tara watched the mesmerised faces of the others. Niamh's eyes grew wide with wonder, and Lucy wrinkled her nose as she breathed in the lovely scent.

It was lucky for them the brownies just happened to be hanging around the area when the torrent washed them away. Or maybe they hadn't just happened to be there. Nothing would surprise her in this strange place.

'Is it okay for us to be here?' asked Niamh. 'I mean, we don't know anyone.'

'All are welcome here that mean well,' squeaked Udell. 'And I am sure you mean well, so you will be welcome. Many folk seek shelter here.'

'We just need help to find out who Niamh really is,' said Tara. 'And we're looking for my father and sister. Will someone be able to help us find them?'

'Princess Gwyn is the one to ask about such things,' said Guido, his voice so much deeper than Udell's. 'I am sure it can be arranged.'

They trotted up a flight of steps towards two great white doors, which had silently begun to open. Tara gingerly stepped between them and into a huge entrance hall. It was breathtaking, with white marble floors and walls, and lit up by hundreds of ivory candles. A fabulous golden fountain stood in the centre, a statue of a dolphin spraying out blue water, which sparkled in the candlelight. Udell told them this had been a present from the merrows, the water people of Iwernia. On the other side of the fountain, a grand staircase stretched upwards. To the left were two tall, white, double doors edged with gilt.

Tara jumped as Udell banged on a brass gong, which stood to the side of them, instantly two people appeared through the white doors, a man and a woman. They were human size, though not very tall and had short, spiky, silver hair, snub noses, soft full lips, long pointed ears, pale skin and violet eyes. Both wore long silken tunics tied around the middle, the man in light brown and the woman in apple green. They briefly bowed their heads.

'I am Avery,' said the man, 'and this is my wife, Sibéal. We are the guardians of this palace and offer our apologies for not being here to greet you after your long journey.'

Tara hesitated, not knowing what to do, then tentatively bowed back. 'That's all right, we weren't expecting it,' she said and introduced everyone.

'We are about to have our evening meal,' said Sibéal pleasantly. 'First you should change out of those wet clothes and your friend needs to be put to bed, I can see she is unwell.'

Avery clapped his hands and two more people with similar looks came and took Lucy from Zalen, who shrank back to his normal size, immediately falling to the ground. Avery offered him his hand and pulled him up. 'Greetings Zalen, we meet again. I see you are not in the company of your mistress...Queen Marvaanagh?'

'Er...no indeed. I – I met these...er...these children and could see they required help so brought them here.'

'Then you did the right thing,' said Sibéal smiling. 'Do follow me, and I will show you all to your rooms.'

Tara smiled back at Sibéal. Now they were finally in a safe and friendly place, they could relax for a while. Perhaps all their problems would be resolved while they were here and they could all go back home.

'Would you stay here, Zalen, I wish to speak with you further,' asked Avery. But it was more of an order than a request.

Zalen nodded and looked resigned, as if not surprised at all he had to stay behind. Tara felt sorry for him, she had a feeling he was in trouble. Who was this Queen Marvaanagh Avery spoke about? Zalen was her servant that was clear. Why hadn't he told them about this? She would certainly be asking him more about it later.

They all followed Sibéal up the majestic marble staircase. Each stair, Tara noticed, had strips of gilding down its sides. Carved into the oak stair rails were ornate leaves tipped with more glistening gold.

Sibéal led them to a number of rooms on the first floor. She gave Lucy and Niamh a room together saying she thought they'd like to share. She showed Tara to the room next to them.

A young girl with spiky white hair came along the hallway and smiling followed Tara into her room.

'I hope this is to your liking,' she said.

'It's enormous!' exclaimed Tara, rapidly taking in the beauty of it all, but her eyes fell back to a magnificent solid oak, four-poster bed, which dominated the room. Like the stair rail, the posts were carved with elaborate leaves. A silken, silver bedspread covered the bed, embroidered with hundreds of tiny flowers in violet and golden yellow. The canopy overhead matched perfectly. A large violet woollen rug covered the marble floor and diaphanous, silver-filigreed curtains, floated at the window.

Sibéal opened a door to reveal a splendid lilac bathroom, complete with everything she might need.

'You will find dry clothing over there in the wardrobe.' Sibéal pointed to a cupboard.

They moved through to Jared's room, Tara went too, as she was curious. It wasn't as elaborate or feminine as Tara's room, but she supposed he wouldn't complain about that. It also had an oak four-poster bed, though without drapes. A plain green cover lay over the bed, and a matching rug on the floor. Jared was more than happy with it.

'Is there somewhere for Leanne to sleep?' asked Jared. He

spoke to empty space. 'No, you can't sleep in here with me.'

'Yes, I will see to it,' said Sibéal, coming into the room.

Tara blushed and gritted her teeth. 'He's been charmed —'

'I understand, do not worry. Your sisters are being cared for so please relax. Zira will be around should you need her.' Sibéal indicated the young girl that had followed them.

Tara went back to her own room, closed the door and headed straight to the wardrobe to find hanging, a shimmering, gauzy nightdress and silken day robes in various shades, similar to those Sibéal and Avery wore. Tara was pleased as her own clothes, ruined in the floodwaters, resembled rags. The nightdress reminded her of the lovely, but sinister, gossamer glamour dress, she had worn in the fairy ring and a cold shiver ran through her. Time for a bath, she thought.

Tara went through to the bathroom to fill the tub, but couldn't find any taps. Looking up she saw nothing, just a lamp, and searching beneath the tub, Tara could find no way of filling it. There must be something that makes it work, thought Tara, or why would it be here.

She ran her hands along the inside of tub and it instantly began to fill with fragrant water. Tara jumped in fright, hoping it would stop when full. Thankfully, it did, and she had a long refreshing soak. She resisted the urge to go under the water. She'd had enough for one day.

Back in the bedroom, Tara chose an aqua-blue, silk robe. It was incredibly soft as it floated down over her, like a hundred butterfly wings against her skin.

She had just finished dressing when Niamh ran into the room. She was wearing a nightdress.

'Isn't it brilliant! Wow! Look at your room! Ours is amazing too. We're not going down to eat. Sibéal says we can eat in our room because Lucy needs to warm up. There's a light elf looking after us, her name is Zira. Come and look.'

So that's what Avery and Sibéal were, thought Tara, light

elves. How many more fae folk would they get to meet? She was sure there were many more, they would need to learn to recognise who was who.

'I'll be there in a sec,' she said. Going to the mirror, she picked up a comb made from iridescent shell, and ran it through her wet hair. There was no way to dry it, so she followed Niamh back to her room.

Lucy lay wrapped up warm and in bed. Jared was sitting by her side still in his own clothes, though his face was clean and his hair shone. Zira the elf girl was busy picking up Lucy's wet clothes.

'You okay, Lucy?' asked Tara, going to the bed and sitting on the other side.

'Yes, I'm just a bit cold still. You saved me, Tara. I might have drowned. It was horrible in the water.'

'It was the stag that saved us, but you were very brave, Lucy.'

'Not as brave as you.' Lucy gave her a hug. 'You didn't have to go in the water with me, you could have saved yourself.'

Tara was embarrassed, she felt like a fraud. How could she tell Lucy it wasn't so much she was brave, more that she knew it would be all right? That she was at home in the water and something, she didn't know what, had compelled her to let go of the handrail and drop in. No one would understand or believe her. When she thought about it, she had never been afraid of water. But to have no fear of such a powerful surge was hard even for her to understand, so how could she explain it to someone else. Better to let them think her brave.

Sibéal arrived at the door with two more light elves carrying trays of food. 'Please join us in the dining hall,' she said to Tara and Jared.

They followed her down the great staircase and into an enormous dining hall. Avery stood waiting for them at the door. A long table stretched down the middle of the room and an assortment of fae folk sat around it, perhaps forty or fifty in all.

The hum of voices filtered through to them along with delicious aromas that caused Tara to feel faint with hunger. She could think of nothing better right now than to have a proper meal. They had used up so much energy with all the walking and the struggle in the river. A measly sandwich had not been enough. When she thought about it, if it wasn't for Niamh and Lucy cleverly thinking of bringing food, they wouldn't even have had that.

'Would you please follow me,' said Avery.

Jared pushed Tara forward, his eyes on the array of food displayed on countless silver dishes down the centre of the table. Avery smiled.

'Thank you,' said Tara, throwing Jared a stern look and pulling back to stand next to Avery again. He offered her his arm and led them to the top of the table. All gazes fell on them, curious to see the human guests, the hum of voices steadily dying away as she and Jared passed.

'Do not worry,' assured Avery. 'You are safe here with us. Relax and enjoy the food.'

He pulled out a chair for Tara, and Sibéal indicated to Jared a chair to the side of her.

Tara noticed an excited wave of whispers begin to travel around the table. Did they regard her and Jared as strange too? And that was why they were so interested in them?

Looking around, Tara recognised light elves and brownies, but there was a variety of other strange folk too. Guido and Udell were sitting halfway along the table, close to a group of curious beings with pale skin and golden hair, and several pint-sized wizened old men with beards down to their feet. Some of the fae folk looked similar to Niamh with ebony hair and dark blue eyes.

'Is it all right if Leanne sits with us?' asked Jared.

Tara glowered at him. This was so embarrassing! Why couldn't he just be normal? But that was never going to happen.

Avery smiled and motioned to a young male elf. 'Can you

please bring a chair, we have an extra guest.'

The elf brought the chair and Jared pulled it up to the table. Tara couldn't believe he could do this to her. He actually believed there was someone there.

The food distracted her as it looked and smelled delicious, with a variety of strange items along with meat, vegetables, fruit and some lovely little savoury cakes.

'Please help yourselves to food,' said Avery, seeing Tara was hesitant. 'It is perfectly safe to eat it. The palace is neutral magically. There are no enchantments here.'

Jared immediately helped himself to the meat and Tara blushed with embarrassment.

Sibéal smiled. 'When you are growing – hunger is never far away.' She reached for a dish of mixed vegetables and offered them to her.

Tara nodded in agreement. She had to admit Jared must be starving too. Forcing a smile, she took the spoon and served herself and taking the dish she offered them to Jared in a token of understanding. She was about to put the dish back on the table when she hesitated, and sighing spooned some onto the dish in front of Jared's imaginary friend. Maybe she should show the light elves she too could rise above all this silliness, just like them.

When everyone had sufficient food, Avery turned his attention to Tara. 'I have placed you next to me, as I need to talk to you both.'

Tara felt worried. What did Avery want to talk to them about? He was frowning and looked serious.

'I believe you ran into some grislic goblins earlier?' Avery continued.

'Yes, we did,' said Tara, rather startled. She was amazed. How could he know that? Then she remembered Zalen would have told him. She suddenly realised Zalen wasn't at the table. Where could he be? Perhaps he had left already, but surely he would have said goodbye.

'They are interested in Niamh,' Avery declared, his voice matter of fact. 'The grislics often hide out in the forest that surrounds the palace. I am sorry they bothered you. They can be such a nuisance.'

'Why do you let them stay around here?' asked Jared.

'Vrogoly Palace is a neutral place in the Realm of Wiltunscire. All are welcome here good or bad, as negative magic does not work inside these walls and grounds. You are safe here from them, so do not worry. They are too ashamed of their own behaviour to venture inside.'

Tara had questions of her own. 'Why do you think they're interested in Niamh?' She didn't want to ask was it because she was of royal blood, because even in her thoughts it sounded silly.

'I cannot answer that right now,' answered Avery. 'You will need to take care. Watch over her. Do not venture outside the palace perimeters alone. In the morning, you can speak to Princess Gwyn. She is eating in her rooms tonight as she is tired after speaking to your friend, Zalen the spriggan. She is of great age.'

Ahh, thought Tara, so he was still around somewhere.

'How do you find the Realm of Wiltunscire?' asked Sibéal.

Tara tried not to think of the grislics, horrible things. If it wasn't for them, the realm wouldn't be half so scary. Sylvia's face popped into her mind and she shook it away. She needed to think of something positive, after all, there was the stag...and Hylda, they had only wanted to help. 'Well...it's interesting,' she said, deciding to be tactful. Avery and Sibéal both laughed at this and even Tara had to smile.

'Is there anything you wish to ask,' questioned Sibéal.

Tara thought about it. 'Who are the people who look similar to Niamh? I mean the ones with the black, curly hair.'

'They are dark elves,' answered Sibéal.

'Is there a big difference between light and dark elves apart from the hair colour and skin tone,' asked Tara, curious.

'Well,' said Sibéal and smiled. 'We light elves prophesise. We are wiser and see future events. Dark elves have more, let us say, practical magical skills, they tend to be impulsive.'

Tara thought about it, so if Niamh was a dark elf she must have magical skills for sure. Zalen had suggested it too, so must have known.

Avery asked about the world of humans. She and Jared told them about their school and hobbies, Jared about football and Tara about her swimming. The other folk at the table had gone back to talking among themselves, although from time to time they glanced at their new guests.

Every so often Tara received an encouraging smile from a young elf or brownie and gradually began to relax, until to her surprise, she noticed the plate of Jared's imaginary friend was now empty. Jared must have eaten it too. He had such a big appetite. Luckily no one noticed. Anyway, it was better not to waste food she reasoned and surprised herself for wanting to make excuses for Jared.

After everyone had finished, the folk began to get up from the table to help clear dishes. 'We'll help,' said Tara looking meaningfully at Jared.

'All guests help in return for the hospitality, but not you...not tonight. You have been through much trauma,' said Sibéal in a motherly way. 'You are tired and should get some rest. In the morning you can breakfast in your rooms and the princess will call you when she is ready to talk to you.'

Jared and Tara thanked Avery and Sibéal and made their own way back to their rooms. They checked in on Niamh and Lucy. Lucy was already asleep. Saying goodnight, Tara went to her own room and changing into the lovely nightdress, she jumped straight into her bed and snuggled down. She yawned, what a day it had been, they had done so much, been through so much. Goodness knew what the next day would have in store.

Chapter Twelve

Tara woke from a dreamless sleep confused at where she was. Remembering, she lay still for a while admiring the embroidered canopy above her. What was happening back at home? Mum and Uncle Fergus must be worried out of their minds. Had they called the police? How long had they been gone, she pondered, two nights and a day? How would they get home again? Perhaps Uncle Fergus guessed where they had gone. After all, he had told them the story about the changeling. It was also possible he didn't have any idea at all and thought it was just a story. Somehow, she didn't think so.

There was a knock on the door and Zira entered with a large tray. A tantalising smell of fresh warm bread drifted towards her. Zira put the breakfast on a table at the side of the bed. She removed a cloth to reveal a rainbow coloured glass filled with fruit juice, along with pear, strawberries, orange segments and strange magenta coloured fruit she didn't recognise. Bread rolls, a small block of butter and a bowl of strawberry jam completed the feast.

Tara heartily thanked Zira who was opening the curtains and window. Again it was sunny, a fresh breeze drifted in causing the delicate curtains to blow into the room like gossamer faery wings.

Zira came back, smiled at her and said, 'I am Princess Gwyn's personal assistant. She will see you after you have breakfasted and dressed. I will come back to show you the way.'

'Er...er...th-thank you, Zira,' stuttered Tara, embarrassed at the special treatment.

'You are most welcome, Tara,' said Zira. She smiled as she left the room. Tara tucked into breakfast. Everything she tasted was scrumptious and she found her first breakfast in bed when she wasn't sick a satisfying experience. She wondered what the day would bring. In one way it was exciting, but in another…

After she washed, she chose to dress in a sea green, ankle length silk tunic. Her own clothes had been taken away and hadn't been returned. She found silken slippers to match, which seemed to hug her feet as soon as she put them on, moulding themselves to fit. Leaving her hair loose, hanging down her back, she decided to go to see if Niamh and Lucy were ready.

'We had breakfast in bed,' said Niamh, brightly, as she opened the door when Tara knocked. She looked vibrant in a lilac silken dress, and Lucy, in a delicate pale blue, had colour in her cheeks. Niamh grinned. 'I can't wait to see Princess Gwyn.' She turned to the mirror to braid her long hair. Lucy went to help.

'I'm going to see if Jared is ready. I bet he's still asleep. Stay here, Niamh, you mustn't go outside alone.'

'Oh, don't fuss, I'm not going anywhere.'

Tara knocked on Jared's door several times. 'Are you ready?' she called.

'Er…yeah.'

'Are you going to let me in then?'

With a grunt, he opened the door. 'I feel so stupid in this get up. Someone has taken my clothes.'

Tara burst out laughing and a smile broke out on Jared's face. Dressed in a short russet tunic, with beige trousers and long brown boots, he looked sheepish. He thumped her playfully on the arm.

'I suppose it could be worse,' he said, opening the wardrobe and taking out a long burgundy tunic similar to the one that Tara wore. 'I could be wearing a dress!'

They were both laughing when Zira appeared at the door. 'Princess Gwyn is ready to see you now.'

They both put on serious faces and collecting the others, they followed Zira up three flights of stairs to the end of a corridor, stopping outside two immense white doors. Opening them, she led the way in. They followed her in silence, not knowing what to expect.

Zira stood aside to reveal a living room, more cosy than luxurious, with quaint old-fashioned chairs upholstered in tapestry. They had a similar chair at home in Uncle Fergus's study. A merry log fire burned in a large fireplace and dotted about the room were various small tables and plants. In a chair next to the fire sat an exceedingly old woman. Her skin was lined, yet Tara could still see her faded beauty. She wore her thick and luxuriant silver hair in a chignon and was dressed simply in the same shade of lilac as Niamh. Tara had expected her to be wearing something much more elaborate.

'Come closer children,' she said as they hung back by the door. Her voice sounded young and musical, belying her great age.

Tara pushed Niamh to the front. They stood by the chair as Princess Gwyn appraised them, first Niamh and then Tara, she nodded to Jared and Lucy. She turned back to Tara and smiled, a look of satisfaction spreading across her features.

'So you have come to visit us.' Her sapphire eyes grew bright and inquisitive.

Tara didn't know what to say to this, as it wasn't strictly true. She decided to tell the princess how and why they came through the gateway into the Realm of Wiltunscire, and how they eventually arrived at the palace. She did this as simply as possible.

Princess Gwyn listened intently, nodding from time to time, her expression grave. 'An interesting story. I am afraid I know nothing for certain about this,' said Princess Gwyn when Tara had finished. 'But telling you what I suspect will only put you in more danger.'

Tara's eyes widened at the word *danger*. Still she wanted, needed even, to know something...anything...that would help her understand what their being in the land of the fae was all about.

The princess seemed to read her mind. 'It is better for you to unravel all the mystery yourselves as there is indeed danger, *grave danger*, ahead. This has been foreseen. Knowing too much will make you more fearful and that will put you at risk.'

'What can you tell us? We would be grateful for anything,' asked Tara. She had a feeling Princess Gwyn was reluctant to tell them anything. After all they had been through, they could take more than she thought they could – she was sure.

Princess Gwyn pondered on this for a while before nodding. 'All right then.' She looked at Niamh. 'Come here, child and hold out your left wrist.'

Niamh stepped forward.

'A pretty bracelet, Niamh, can you remove it?'

Niamh took it off and held it out to her. Princess Gwyn shook her head. 'Put it on again, my dear, and hold out your wrist again.'

Niamh shrugged her shoulders, put the bracelet back on and held out her arm. Princess Gwyn took her wrist and tried to remove it, but clearly couldn't.

'Tara, can you please try to remove Niamh's bracelet?'

Tara tried, but couldn't do it either. Lucy and Jared both tried.

'That's strange,' said Niamh.

'What does it mean?' asked Tara.

Princess Gwyn frowned and looked gravely at Niamh. 'If it is what I think it is – it will protect you from death. And you must promise me, Niamh, never to take it off again no matter how terrible the circumstances. This is a promise you *must* not break. Taking it off could cause all of your deaths. Without it, you are vulnerable. With it you have power.'

'Yes, all right, if it's important,' said Niamh, looking quizzically at the others.

Tara thought this strange. How could a bracelet given to Niamh by Uncle Fergus protect her? Was it just a coincidence it had magical powers? If it was, Niamh was very lucky Uncle Fergus found it. Maybe he'd discovered it on one of his digs, perhaps even at Stonehenge. The thought struck her the bracelet may well have been with Niamh when she was changed. Uncle Fergus may have found it in the house and put it away. Then for some reason gave it to Niamh on her birthday. The more Tara pondered on this the more she thought there was some truth in it. Uncle Fergus must know about the changing...the gateway. Just because Mum had forgotten, it didn't mean Uncle Fergus had.

'Now,' began Princess Gwyn, 'the answers you seek lie at Caer Searesby, a castle which lies south of here where the five rivers meet. I have long suspected something untoward there. You must be extremely wary of Queen Marvaanagh who lives at the castle. She is the chief guardian of the young Princess Donella of Wiltunscire, my great niece and the heir to this realm.

Queen Marvaanagh! That was it thought Tara. Avery had mentioned Zalen was her servant, so she did have something to do with all this. Zalen must be escaping from her. What was more; if Princess Donella had a guardian, she must be a child.

Niamh must have been thinking the same thing as she asked, 'Princess Donella wouldn't be eleven years old with strawberry-blonde hair, would she?'

'No my dear, she is sixteen years old with black hair rather like yours. And just as I am concerned for your safety, I am also concerned for hers. I feel there is grave danger ahead for you all and Queen Marvaanagh is at the heart of it. She is indeed the most powerful person of the three realms now that Donella's parents are gone, and attacks on the Realm of Dumnonia take up her uncle, King Branwalather's time.' Princess Gwyn's face set into a grim expression. 'Donella shows no predisposition towards magical abilities like her father and mother did before her, so she is at risk. I am hoping that when she finds Craebh Ciuil, her mother's wand, it will all change. But the wand has not yet presented itself and will only do so when the true owner is ready for it and in great need, remember that. No one else must take it the first time it appears except the *rightful* owner, or it will disappear and you will all be left in danger.'

If Princess Donella was the rightful owner, thought Tara, only she must take Craebh Ciuil. She must make sure no one else did. She hoped the wand would present itself if Princess Donella were in need, it sounded as if she could do with it.

'Do we really have to go to this castle, Caer Searesby?' Tara asked. 'It sounds like a dangerous place.'

'Yes, you must speak with Donella to find some of the answers to your conundrum. But first you will need to seek help from the Mordanta to help you gain access to Caer Searesby.'

'The Mordanta, who are they?' asked Niamh.

'They are three queens, Niamh, some say witches – who are never apart from one another. They are as one and will help you. To reach them you will need to go by the leys, be warned though, this is an exceptionally hazardous way to travel.'

Tara glanced at Lucy who had paled. But she needn't have worried.

'Lucy, you are not fit enough to go, after your ordeal in the water,' declared Princess Gwyn. 'It would be better if you and Niamh only travel as far as the gateway. Then wait for Tara and Jared to return.'

Tara exchanged looks with Jared. No way was she going anywhere alone with him! She'd rather go by herself. Straight away, she knew it wasn't true. It wouldn't be something she would want to face without support.

'Okay, we'll go,' said Jared, without hesitation. 'What do we have to do?'

Tara had no choice, she had to brave it out. If she refused, everyone would think she was afraid. 'What are...erm...er... leys?' she asked.

'They are magical tunnels, which can carry you swiftly from gateway to gateway in a very short time. But they are narrow and hold many hazards, such as sharp stones and protruding tree roots.' She paused. 'Realm folk have been killed travelling them. Still, the purer your purpose the less likely this is to happen. And your purpose is pure enough…still it must be your own choice.'

'Do we really need the Mordanta to help us?' asked Niamh.

'Yes, I am afraid so.'

Tara thought about it. They could just continue on to Caer Searesby without help and hope for the best. But having travelled through the forest and met many dangers already, they needed all the help they could get. Tara felt safe at the palace, but they couldn't stay forever. She didn't relish travelling at high speed down narrow tunnels, but they would have to go, so it really wasn't a choice.

'How do we find these tunnels…leys?'

'Through a gateway.'

'What! We've just come from there!' exclaimed Jared, earning a hard look from Tara.

Princess Gwyn wasn't fazed. 'There is more than one gateway. You need to travel north, so the best gateway would be at Rath Sarog, the home of Humbert the Jotunn, though it is a little tricky to gain entry. You take the path going south towards Five Rivers, at a certain point, you will need to backtrack northwards by way of the leys to reach Caer Sidi where the Mordanta reside. However difficult it is, it will still be quicker than travelling on foot. The sooner you are on your way to Caer Searesby the less time others have to plot against you. I am sure Zalen the spriggan who accompanied you here, will be more than happy to show you the way.'

'Will this Humbert person let us through okay,' asked Tara.

'Yes, with careful handling. He may well ask for a fee. Although once he is your friend, he is a friend for life. You need to request he take care of Lucy and Niamh while you travel north. They will be safe with him.'

'Thank you,' said Tara, she could see the princess grew weary, but needed to ask a couple more questions. 'Can you tell me if you have heard of a human man coming to this realm ten years ago? He came here at the same time as my baby sister was taken.'

'No, no my dear, I am afraid not. Humans take on the characteristics of the fae if they have lived here for a time and it becomes difficult to tell them apart. So even if they were here, your human sister and father would blend in with the realm population.' She picked up a glass from her side table next to her chair and took a sip of water before continuing.' However, I can tell you one last thing, which may help you. Niamh...your magical powers will strengthen the longer you are in this realm. Believe in them to take best advantage.' She turned towards Tara. 'Tara, you too have powers passed down through your ancestry, strength of mind, powerful intuition, and other gifts. Be strong. Use that strength of mind, as you have done already. Follow your intuition, it will serve you well.'

'Thanks for all your help,' said Niamh.

Princes Gwyn smiled wearily, took Niamh's hands, and after looking carefully at her for several seconds, kissed her on each cheek. 'Take care, my dear child. You may well be the future of this realm.'

The future of this realm, what did that mean, pondered Tara. Why couldn't they just be told what was going on? She knew she couldn't ask now, hopefully they would learn more before they left the palace.

Zira gestured to them to leave the room, opening the door for them. As they stepped into the hallway, Princess Gwyn spoke again. 'There is a reception tonight in the entrance hall and gardens. It is the state visit from King Branwalather of Dumnonia and the formal signing of the betrothal of Princess Donella and Prince Mawgan of Dumnonia, though obviously Donella will not be attending, which is *very* strange. However, Prince Mawgan will be there. Be alert. I will see you all there. Tomorrow you must leave for Rath Sarog.'

Princess Gwyn closed her eyes. Zira smiled and quietly closed the door.

Jared grinned and whispered to Tara, 'Ooh you have magical powers. Are you going to put a spell on me?'

Tara glared at him. 'Niamh would be the one with the magical powers, I just have good intuition. And my intuition is telling me you need to grow up. Princess Gwyn says we're all in danger.' She knew fear must show in her eyes, and looked away.

'We'll be all right, don't worry. We're going to get help aren't we from the Mordanta?' He put his arm around Tara's shoulders then suddenly twisted around. 'Stop nudging me, Leanne,' he said.

Tara shrugged his arm off. 'You'd better go play with your friend.'

'Leanne says, you don't have to be jealous,' said Jared, the expression in his voice innocent as he relayed what Leanne said to him. 'She says I can have more than one friend.'

'Jared! Urgh...oh forget it.' She marched off down the stairs after the others.

Chapter Thirteen

Back in her room, Tara plonked herself down on her bed. She pushed her fingers through her hair. What a twit! What an idiot! What was it with Jared and his stupid imaginary friend? It was pathetic he couldn't be without admirers for even a day, so he'd just invented one! Well, if he wanted to be friends with a shadow instead of her, so be it.

Anyway, she had more important things to worry about – the ley tunnels for instance. Scrambling through a narrow tunnel, one with spiky tree roots, and rocks poking out...

Tara pictured it. In her mind's eye, it was pitch black and they had to feel their way. Jared would be no help of course and there was no way she was going to tell him she was afraid. Well, she wouldn't allow him to take Leanne with him. She had enough to cope with without him acting daft and being distracted all the time.

Tara must have dozed off for a few minutes, she awoke with a start. In her short dream, she had been shooting down through a dark tunnel flat on her back, rather like being on a slide at a theme park. With any luck, that's what it would be like, quick and fun, well apart from the tree roots sticking up and the narrow space. Feeling better, she decided she would go and see what the others were doing.

Niamh opened the door when Tara knocked. Not that she ever knocked on doors at home, but here in the palace, it just seemed appropriate.

'We're just trying on dresses for the reception,' said Niamh excitedly. She opened the door wide to reveal Lucy wearing a pale pink, satin gown, it had an under gown of white with a crisscrossed bodice. Niamh was wearing a long, silky, cream gown, with long tight sleeves, puffed out at the top.

Jared was sitting on a chair. 'Wow fancy dress party or what!'

'You both look great,' said Tara ignoring him. 'I think I'll go and see what might be in my own wardrobe.' She smiled, turned on her heel and left the room as normally as she could, not rushing, not showing her annoyance. They could all be cosy together, what did she care…

Reaching her room, she resisted the urge to slam her door and went straight to the wardrobe to see if she also had a dress to wear. She opened the door and gasped. A beautiful gown hung there. She took it out, running her hand down the rich, dark green velvet.

Excited now, she put it on and looked in the mirror. It reached to the ground, the sleeves long and coming to a point over her hands. It fitted perfectly. She couldn't help smiling. An under gown of white showed through a centre panel, the bodice criss-crossed with matching green ribbons. She just had to show Niamh and Lucy.

When a few moments later Jared opened the bedroom door to her, he gasped.

'You look…er…erm …pretty.' He was wearing a white tunic with an over robe of bronze and black trousers tucked into boots.

'So do you. I mean…look handsome. Leanne around?'

'Nope.'

Tara couldn't help herself. 'Oh, I thought she might have a dress too and be looking like a little princess.'

'She's seven years old, Tara, too young to go to the reception.'

Tara realised Jared was serious – he had no doubt at all he had a seven-year-old fae child following him everywhere. She would just have to learn to ignore it. 'Of course, silly me.' But a note of sarcasm crept into her voice.

Zira appeared at the open door. 'I do hope you like what I chose for you all to wear to the reception,' she said. They all nodded their approval. 'The reception begins at dusk, until then, may I show you around the palace, there are many wonderful things to see.'

'We'll just get changed. We'd love to see around the palace...wouldn't we?' Tara directed this towards the others, who all nodded agreement.

Zira brought them to a delightful inner courtyard, which had a magnificent display of late blooming, cabbage rose bushes, in every imaginable colour. Tara sat down on a cushioned bench by an enchanting glass fountain with intertwining water fairies and set with precious gems. The others joined her.

'Wouldn't this look great in our garden?' enthused Niamh.

'This must be the nicest place in the world,' added Lucy.

Jared pulled a face and put his hands up like a zombie, in a spooky voice he said, 'Enjoy it while you can. Tomorrow we'll be travelling along the dangerous leys to see the mysterious Mordanta.'

The Mordanta, Tara had forgotten about them in her obsession with the ley tunnels. Would they help them? They did sound mysterious; especially the way Princess Gwyn called them by one title, *The Mordanta*, rather than by single names.

'Well, we don't have to worry about that yet,' she said at last. She did worry though. Queen Marvaanagh was certainly at the root of their problems, but it would be hard to avoid her if she lived at Caer Searesby. If Tara was to find her missing sister and her father, they had to speak with Princess Donella. She must know something about it, Princess Gwyn was right. It was strange she couldn't come to her own betrothal signing. Sixteen and getting married though...Tara couldn't imagine it. In three years, she herself would be sixteen. But things were done differently here. Everything was different. In fact, everything was very peculiar.

Niamh gave a little jump of excitement. 'I can't wait for the ball tonight.'

'A ball!' said Lucy, with a dreamy expression. 'Like in Cinderella!'

Jared sniggered. 'Well, I don't think there will be a prince there, silly.'

'Well, in fact there will be – Prince Mawgan,' said Tara. 'That's what the reception, not ball, is all about.'

'Oh yeah, I forgot. See, a prince especially for you, Luce.'

Tara tried not to smile as a rose coloured blush slowly covered Lucy's face and neck. But yes, Prince Mawgan was Donella's betrothed, so he must know something that could help them. She should try to talk to him. The thought of that daunted her. She'd never spoken to a prince before. She laughed to herself, only this morning they had been chatting to a princess. It couldn't be that bad then.

Zira reappeared and suggested they continue with the tour.

They walked through the many passageways. The vastness of the place amazed Tara. They visited staterooms, galleries, more courtyards, and even passed by a great library. The fae folk often stared at Niamh; she was attracting lots of attention. It must be because she looked as if she belonged here, and yet she was a stranger, thought Tara.

Zira pointed out several fae folk species including feeorin, and the strange Scottish water folk, the silkies, with their webbed feet and hands. The water folk fascinated her the most. And as well as silkies, she saw nixies, who were striking, with pale skin, and extraordinary large green eyes and golden hair. Tara remembered them from the dining hall. But the most curious of all were two female merrows from Iwernia who had greeted them. One had looked Tara up and down and given her a broad smile. Tara was mesmerised by their green-tinged fair hair, and webbed fingers so like her own had been while in the river. Zira told them that when in the sea they had fishtails.

Leanne must have been with them on the tour, as Jared kept acting as if someone was jumping on him. Aggravated, he kept pushing her off. Tara ignored him. Just as from now on, she intended to ignore the so-called Leanne.

Lunch was in the great dining hall, again, many fae folk sat around the table. Zira asked them would they like go to the library after they'd eaten. She described it as a place of great knowledge, which she was sure they would find most interesting. The food tasted delicious, and Tara listened into a few conversations, which she was surprised to find were no different from back home. There was much in the way of polite talk of gardening and the weather, the trials of travelling, latest recipes, and which herb was good for what ailment.

After eating and helping clear the dishes, they went straight to the circular library, an immense room. Tara didn't know where to begin. Books lined the walls, from massive volumes to thin pamphlets. They stood in tall bookcases reaching up high to the ceiling. Hundreds of scrolls lay in glass drawers around the perimeter of the room. A number of fae folk sat on the many marble benches at tables leafing through books or perusing charts.

They began by viewing the various portraits, which hung on the walls, and statues and busts that stood on plinths. Some of the images were of past descendants of Princess Gwyn. One portrait in particular interested Tara, as it was the largest and took pride of place in the centre of the library. Zira told her it was Anya, who was once the reigning Queen of the Realm of Wiltunscire, mother of Donella.

The picture captivated Tara. Anya, dainty, slender and graceful, her hair hanging down her back in dark curls, was beautiful. She was young, with only a few laughter lines around her indigo eyes. Indigo eyes just like Niamh's. In fact, Queen Anya looked just like Niamh. It was unsettling. No wonder the fae folk had been staring at Niamh. Tara heard a sharp intake of breath behind her. She turned to see Niamh and Lucy staring open mouthed at the portrait.

'Sh-she looks like me.' The words caught in Niamh's throat. 'What does it mean?'

'If this is your mother, then you must be the younger sister of Princes Donella,' said Tara with confidence.

Jared had joined them. 'Wow…that has to be your mum, Niamh.

Zalen was right, when he had said Niamh had royal blood. He must know more about this than he was letting on. But where was the other baby, Tara's real sister? They already knew no human child lived at the castle, there was only Donella. Perhaps Donella knew where she was. Or maybe it was discovered the babies had been swapped and the human baby was taken somewhere else to be looked after. Now though, no one would recognise her as human. It would make things so much more difficult. They must talk to Donella. She would be sure to help them, and would be so pleased to have her sister back, just as Tara would be so happy to have hers back too. Tara voiced her thoughts to the others.

'Yes, that must be it.' Niamh grinned widely. 'Now I know who I am and where I come from. I just want to go there and meet Donella. This is so exciting. I feel I've come home.'

Everything was changing before Tara's eyes. Niamh suddenly seemed distant from her, no longer *her* sister, but someone else's. It was horrible. Tara felt alone. She wanted to find her dad. She wanted him back and everything to be normal again. *Again*, had it ever been normal? No, for as long as she could remember her family wasn't like other people's families. Her dad was missing and her mother had mental health problems. Uncle Fergus was great, but he was different somehow, the neighbours thought him eccentric. Sometimes they called him 'that hippy fellow'.

'There is a history of the Realm of Wiltunscire. You may view it if you wish,' suggested Zira, coming up behind them.

'We would love to, thank you, Zira,' said Tara, thinking they should learn as much as possible about the Realm of Wiltunscire.

Zira took them to the history section and unlocking a cupboard, she drew out a brown leather book so large Jared had to help her lift it. The cover was well worn and embossed with gold. They placed it on a marble table and she opened it. Tara gasped, it was beautifully hand written in gold ink and skilfully illustrated. Thick, it would take ages to read the whole history. Deep inside her, she hoped it might reveal something of the mysteries concerning Niamh.

'Can we see the more recent history please,' she requested.

Zira opened the book halfway; the pages were empty. 'They are for future recordings,' she said. She turned back a few pages. 'Avery is in charge of recording events.'

Zira turned the book towards them. They all pushed and pulled to get a look.

'I think Niamh and I should look first,' Tara said.

Zira kept silent as she and Niamh read all about the three realms of this part of the Otherworld. Queen Anya had ruled the Realm of Wiltunscire, Queen Marvaanagh ruled the Realm of Glastenning, while King Branwalather ruled the Realm of Dumnonia. Tara read that when the young Anya had become queen she had soon after married King Edmwnd who came from *Ynys Dywyll* to the northwest of the realms.

A year later, Anya gave birth to a baby daughter whom they called Donella. The young queen and king happily ruled, until rumours of a plot against them emerged. It told of how Donella was kidnapped while on a state visit to Glastenning with her parents and while searching for her, the queen and king became trapped on Ynys Is. No one knew how, the information about it was sketchy.

It was Queen Marvaanagh who had found Donella safe and well on one of the islands of her realm of Glastenning and having brought her to safety, had become her guardian, much to the gratitude of the folk of Wiltunscire, who still had a future queen in Donella. It seemed before this, hostility existed between the two realms. A truce ensued once Queen Marvaanagh came to Wiltunscire.

Tara was disappointed; nowhere did it mention another daughter. It never even mentioned exactly how long ago Donella parents became trapped. How annoying. This was becoming more puzzling than ever. She exchanged glances with Niamh and Niamh sadly shook her head. They didn't want to discuss it in front of Zira so waited until they got back to Niamh and Lucy's room.

'Well, I still think you're right, Tara,' agreed Niamh. 'I fit in here somewhere. Maybe people don't want to talk about the missing baby for some reason. Maybe two children went missing and they only found one, Donella.'

'Yes, that's right,' said Lucy. 'Maybe, they thought she'd never be found, and wanted to forget all about it.'

'You are of royal blood, Niamh, we know that,' decided Tara. And you look like Queen Anya. You must be related to Donella and she must know something. If only we knew your real name, it would help enormously.'

Out of the window, they could see a lot of activity going on. They watched as some men erected a number of colourful striped tents on the large lawn beyond the rose garden.

At last, a group of people on horses came down the driveway. One figure stood out – a large man with white hair. His black cloak fluttered behind him in the wind as he rode swiftly, ahead of everyone else. Close behind him rode a younger man, with dark hair that glittered gold in the sun, this must be the prince, thought Tara, and the other man must be his uncle, King Branwalather. A number of soldiers accompanied them. They wore short capes and carried swords. In turn, an entourage followed them.

The king and prince dismounted, servants appeared and led away the horses. Prince Mawgan looked up and caught Tara's eye. She jumped back embarrassed.

'Oh no, he saw me watching!' she cried in horror.

The others just laughed. Tara blushed.

Chapter Fourteen

Donella paced her room, wondering what to do. Caer Searesby was alive with activity. Her Aunt Marvaanagh had doubled her guard of grislic goblins. They scurried here and there following her biddings.

Donella had been assigned a personal maid who hung around her chamber. She had never had a personal maid. Even though she was the heir to the realm, her aunt left her to fend for herself except for on state occasions.

Immediately the maid had appeared at her door, Donella knew she now had a guard. There must be some way to escape her and to discover what was going on. Whatever it was, she had a growing feeling it involved her. Why else would her aunt confine her? Why else did no one tell her what was going on? Whatever it was, it was momentous. Donella was sure it had something to do with the children her Aunt Marvaanagh wanted to kill. Her one consolation was that Mawgan had somehow managed to speak with them and warn them.

Donella felt she had two choices, stay put and attempt to get to the secret passageway to try to discover what was going on, or escape Caer Searesby and make her way to her Aunt Gwyn. She felt the first option was more viable as so many goblins guarded the castle now, she would not get far. Marvaanagh had an army in the Realm of Glastenning, but she was wise enough not to use it and raise the suspicions of the realm folk. So goblins it was that now overran the castle like a swarm of beetles.

Donella made a plan for that very same night. As soon as her maid fell asleep she would make her way to the passageway. She would have to do this in darkness; she was pleased she had thought to leave the lamp and tinderbox just inside the concealed doorway.

Later that night as soon as she was sure the maid was asleep, Donella left her room. She had changed from her long skirts into breeches and a tunic she used for riding; she always found this clothing so much easier to move in. Once in the gallery, the waning moon glowed full enough to throw some light through the windows, and in no time at all, Donella reached the secret passageway. Lighting her lamp, she crept down the stairs.

She emerged in the buttery, deciding to leave her lamp behind and proceed in the dark. She passed the kitchens gratified there was not a soul in sight. Everyone was in bed. Through the window, she could see guards scurrying up and down the inner and outer ward battlements.

Donella had decided to head towards the east tower where her Aunt Marvaanagh had her chamber. She had just reached the first landing, when she heard footsteps and quickly concealed herself behind a pillar. Her aunt swept past her in her white night clothes, like a ghost in the night. She carried a dimmed lamp. Donella waited until she passed before following.

Marvaanagh descended the staircase, passed by the great hall and on towards the north tower. Donella's parents had used the chambers there, and Marvaanagh forbade Donella to enter them. Marvaanagh had showed them to her once years ago, but as nothing appeared to remain that belonged to her parents, Marvaanagh having probably disposed of it or stored it all, the rooms seemed empty and cold. Donella had been happy not to go there again. But if there was not anything of interest there, why would Marvaanagh even want to go to the chambers? There must be a good reason and Donella wanted to know what that was.

Keeping well behind, Donella followed, her slippers making little noise on the stone stairs. As soon as she stepped into the hallway, she saw she was right. She watched as Marvaanagh entered her parent's chambers, closing the door behind her.

Donella crept up and peered through the keyhole, but it was too dark for her to see. Putting her ear to the door, she heard a scraping noise as if something was being lifted and put down again.

Marvaanagh began to utter some strange words. Magic, she was using magic, thought Donella. She heard a curse, something slammed against the wall. Whatever was going on Marvaanagh had been unable to achieve what she wanted. Donella knew at once that she must try to find out what it was her aunt was trying or attempting to do. It must be important, very important.

Donella ran back down the hallway and hid in a laundry cupboard, closing the door just as her aunt came out of the chambers. Donella could hear her heavy breathing as she passed by and feel her radiating vibrations of anger.

As soon as she deemed it safe, Donella went to her parents' chamber. The door was unlocked, but she could see nothing, the room too dark. She would need to return for her lamp. In the distance, Donella heard at least two sets of footsteps and some voices. She decided to come back later, when things had quietened down. It would be a much safer option.

Donella reached her room without problem. Putting her ear against the maid's bedchamber, which was actually a storeroom attached to her own rooms, she could hear her slow steady breathing. She sat on her bed and rested for a few minutes, gathering her thoughts. She had strong intuition, which had never let her down. Fear crept up her spine spreading throughout her body – she was in danger. Suddenly she felt very alone, and she tried not to think what it was like for her parents, frozen forever, on Ynys Is.

* * *

Tara, Niamh, Lucy and Jared, stood watching the preparations for the rest of the afternoon. The prince and king had come into the palace with four soldiers. The rest of the soldiers, with the remaining entourage, had walked over to the tents.

Later they all dressed in their lovely new clothes. Music drifted up the stairs. Glancing at each other Niamh and Lucy giggled. Tara hid her own glee at living a fairytale. She could only wish it would all end happily ever after, but this was all too real, she had to remember that. Real and perilous and they had to be on their guard at all times. Yet going to meet a prince dressed in the most beautiful clothing she had ever worn, for tonight anyway, she would allow herself to enjoy.

They strolled downstairs, into the main entrance hall, which was lit up with hundreds of candles. The doors to the garden stood wide open. Tara could see the fireflies darting about and lanterns hanging in the trees. The palace hummed with the voices of the fae folk standing around chatting, the whole scene was colourful and bright with everyone dressed in their finery.

A group of men and women played music by the fountain. Tara recognised them as merrows. She wandered closer towards them and was taken aback. One of them wore a yellow shirt and didn't have green hair like the others, but silver, and he looked a bit like Uncle Fergus. He was half turned away from her, so she couldn't see his face. She spotted Zira.

'Zira,' she said, patting her arm to attract her attention. 'Those men playing music, who are they?'

'They are merrows, they offered to provide the entertainment. Why, is there something wrong?'

Tara looked back – the silver-haired merrow had gone. She must have been imagining things. 'No, nothing…it's all right…never mind.'

'You look lovely, Tara,' said Zira, a big smile lighting up her dainty face. 'I think I chose well for you.

Tara blushed, she wasn't used to compliments, she thought Zira looked far more striking. Dressed in a pale pink flowing dress, she resembled an angel with her short white hair threaded with silver and her ears just pointed enough to identify her as a white elf.

Niamh and Lucy caught up with them.

'Zira, are you coming out in the garden?' asked Lucy.

'Yes I would love to, thank you.'

The three sauntered out through the great white doors.

Jared who had been inspecting the food, walked over to Tara. 'Come on, let's go have a gander.'

'We need to find Prince Mawgan.'

'Well, he's not in here, so we may as well look in the garden.'

Tara had to agree. She nodded.

Out in the garden it truly was the land of the fae. The glow of lights from the fireflies and lanterns gave it an ethereal look. An exquisite scent emanated from the roses. They wandered around the rose garden for a while, before taking a path, which led into a hidden garden near the lake. Someone strolled there, it was a man dressed in a black cloak over a bright yellow shirt. He had silver sticky-up hair and a beard.

'Uncle Fergus!' shrieked Tara, recognising the merrow from before, which wasn't a merrow at all…couldn't be. The man carried on walking and disappeared around the next corner.

'Uncle Fergus!' called Tara again. She ran after him around the corner only to find the path had abruptly ended at the lake's edge. There was no one there, just the reflection of the waning moon floating on the surface and a few ripples on the water.

'What's the matter?' asked Jared as he ran to catch up with her. 'Who was that man? Where did he go?'

'You did see him then…I was beginning to think I was seeing things. I don't know where he went, but I thought it was Uncle Fergus. Honestly, he looked just like him. How weird!' She stood there until the rippling subsided.

'What would he be doing here?'

'I really don't know. But I was certain…'

As there was no sign of Prince Mawgan, they set off back towards the palace. Just inside the door, Tara spotted Princess Gwyn talking to someone – a tall, handsome man, with golden streaked, dark hair, the same young man who had seen her looking out of the window...Prince Mawgan. Tara nudged Jared and they walked over. Princess Gwyn wore a rich royal-blue satin gown and she looked a lot less tired than the night before. She moved towards them.

'Greetings children,' she said. 'Are you enjoying yourselves?'

'Yes, thank you,' answered Tara, feeling suddenly shy as the prince appraised her.

Princess Gwyn turned her attention to Prince Mawgan.

'Mawgan, may I present to you, Tara and Jared. They are the human children I spoke to you about.'

'Good evening, Tara...Jared. It is good to meet you both.' He inclined his head and smiled...a real smile decided Tara, one that reached his eyes.

'Good evening. We're glad to meet you too,' said Tara, trying to decide if she should curtsy or something. She settled for a smile. Jared just nodded his head. It was all very awkward, but the prince smiled again and Tara relaxed.

'I must go to speak with your uncle, the king. We must prepare for the signing of the betrothal papers,' said Princess Gwyn. 'I will leave you young people together.'

As they watched Princess Gwyn walk gracefully towards the palace doors, Tara considered what to say, but Mawgan spoke first. 'I am most delighted we have an opportunity to converse,' he said, surprising Tara. 'I have need to speak with you most urgently.'

He wanted to speak to *them*? How did he know who they were, thought Tara?

Mawgan answered her question. 'The Princess Donella requested I speak with you.'

'Princess Donella!' exclaimed Tara. 'How does she know who we are, that we're even here at the palace?'

'Well, it is not that she knows who you are. She has only heard you are here in the Realm of Wiltunscire...three human children and a realm child by all accounts. Do others accompany you?'

'Yes, Niamh and Lucy.'

'Then I believe we should go and seek them out. This message concerns you all.'

Tara smiled her agreement, and led the way to where they had last seen Niamh and Lucy heading. They found them in a walled garden, chasing fireflies. Lucy spotted them first, her eyes widened, causing her to look like a rabbit caught in headlights. She ran in front of the prince and curtsied rather awkwardly, nearly losing her balance.

'Erm...arise, young lady. I am sure there is no need for such formalities.'

'This is Lucy, Jared's sister,' said Tara. 'And this is my sister Niamh. She turned to the prince. 'This is Prince Mawgan.'

Prince Mawgan looked at Niamh, then back at Tara. 'Please, Mawgan will be fine. We can surely drop such terms when alone. Mmm, you look very familiar to me.'

'Yes,' said Tara. 'We've discovered Niamh looks very much like Queen Anya.'

'I was not speaking of Niamh. I was referring to you, Tara.'

'Me!'

'You remind me of someone, though I cannot think who.'

Tara gaped in astonishment. What could it mean? Still, she explained her theory about how Niamh might be Donella's sister.

'I will say that indeed Niamh does resemble Queen Anya, and in fact many of the other nobles, such as Queen Marvaanagh,' said Mawgan when she had finished. 'Niamh is certainly of royal blood, but the family is a large one. And if there is a lost sister, I can assure you, Donella knows nothing of her.'

Disheartened, tears stinging her eyes, which she blinked hurriedly away, Tara tried to sound nonchalant. 'We thought we'd solved the mystery when we came across the portrait of Queen Anya. But it seems not. Surely Donella would know if she had a younger sister of eleven years old. She would be at least six years old when she disappeared ten years ago.'

'I am most sorry to disappoint you. But I would also know of her, as I have known Princess Donella all my life.' Mawgan put his arm around Tara, and taking a soft white handkerchief from his pocket, he wiped her eyes. Tara felt mortified at showing her emotions in front of a stranger…a handsome one at that. But at least thinking that stopped the tears.

'If it is of any help, which I am sure it will not be as it contains a dire warning, Donella requested of me that if I see three human children and a realm child, to inform them they are in imminent danger from her aunt, Queen Marvaanagh. This warning included the spriggan servant Zalen, who must be killed on sight.'

A gasp of astonishment and horror came from them all.

'Zalen! Killed! That's horrible!' said Lucy, shocked.

'I am afraid, that by all accounts, Queen Marvaanagh only wants to have Niamh brought to her alive. And as such, all your lives are in danger.'

All of them killed! Since Tara had first seen the hare by the mound she'd had a feeling of dread that someone or something was after them, wanting to harm them in some way, but kill them…no, it hadn't crossed her mind. Lucy was right. It was horrible. Why would Queen Marvaanagh, who didn't even know them, want to kill them? The thought of the bridge crossed Tara's mind. The collapse could have killed them all, and specifically her and Lucy. It was true. Marvaanagh had already tried to kill them.

'I think Donella herself is in danger,' said Prince Mawgan. 'Now that I have spoken to you, except she does not know it. This puzzle surely involves her too. As soon as I saw you, in my heart I knew. I must get back to her as soon as I can.'

'We're going anyway,' said Niamh, raising her eyebrows questioningly. 'You could come with us. We need to find out what's going on.'

Tara explained they first must go to Rath Sarog and travel the ley to see the Mordanta who would help them. They would then go onto Caer Searesby to speak with Princess Donella.

'The Mordanta?' said Mawgan, his eyes grew wide with astonishment. 'They help few so I am most surprised you are being sent to them. They have been known at times to protect the heirs and rulers of this realm. Indeed, the mystery deepens.'

Many people strolled by now, so they began to walk down one of the many smaller pathways in the garden. Tara told Mawgan about all their experiences, their run in with Sylvia, and the dangers they had faced with the flying rocks and the flash flood that could easily have killed her and Lucy. In turn, Mawgan told them how he came to be betrothed to Donella and how pleased about it they both were, apart from wishing they could wait until they were both a little older. Tara thought it so romantic.

Mawgan explained how soon, several selected people would retire to the stateroom to witness Princess Gwyn signing the papers. King Branwalather would keep one copy, Princess Gwyn another, and the third copy would be returned to Queen Marvaanagh.

In one week hence, they would be married and Donella would at last be Queen of Wiltunscire and Mawgan would be her consort king.

As the named heir of the Realm of Dumnonia, one day he would be king in his own right. If anything happened to Donella and she had not married, Queen Marvaanagh would become Queen of the Realm of Wiltunscire, so would in fact be queen of two realms. A few years ago, that would not have been acceptable to the folk of the realm as they despised her. Now though, they had warmed to her as she had looked after Donella so well.

'That is what worries me,' he said. 'Only Donella stands in the way of Marvaanagh having control of two realms...hmm, much power for one person. I never liked her, but until Donella spoke to me recently, I never thought her capable of murder. Though I must say there are rumours in her own realm, Glastenning, she is capable of great cruelty and she is not well liked among her own people. I had ignored it all until now. Then suddenly, all this great rush to push the marriage through. With so many people around at the wedding from far off realms, it would be a perfect opportunity to arrange an assassination as there would be great confusion. But perhaps my imagination is running away with me.'

Tara shook her head. 'No, it all makes sense now. Niamh must be an heir too. She has to be.'

'Yes, I must be,' agreed Niamh. 'I can feel it. It's hard to explain, all I know is this has something to do with me. It was seeing the picture of Queen Anya I suppose...I knew then, deep inside me.'

'Indeed this could be true,' said Mawgan. 'There are things we do not know. Queen Marvaanagh has not yet been named officially as heir. Each heir has to be first recognised and accepted by a committee of realm folk elders. After Queen Anya and King Edmwnd became trapped on Ynys Is, the Princess Donella was named as heir. At her coronation, a new heir will be put forward and accepted or rejected. If the committee rejected Queen Marvaanagh, it would be my uncle who would be named as heir instead, unless Donella has a child of her own. As it is, because of the troubles in Dumnonia, the elders would most likely choose Queen Marvaanagh in the absence of a new baby. Especially as they bear no grudge against her themselves.'

'And if Queen Marvaanagh wants Niamh, she must be a threat somehow. We are all a threat to her plans in fact, even you.' Tara rubbed her forehead. 'If something happened to your uncle and you, then Marvaanagh would rule Dumnonia too...wouldn't she?'

'Yes, indeed, that is very true. The plot thickens. Could

Marvaanagh be planning to rule all three realms? She must indeed be trying to kill us all – and almost succeeded killing you and Lucy. I had not considered that I too was in any danger or my uncle.'

Tara sighed. 'I just wish we could piece together the whole puzzle.'

Mawgan patted her shoulder. 'At least we are getting somewhere with it. Try not to worry. The rest of the answers lie at Caer Searesby with Donella and the sooner we go back there, the better.'

Tara decided she liked Mawgan. Charming, handsome and intelligent, actually, he was everything she thought a prince should be. Lucy was besotted with him. She hardly spoke, but stared at him constantly, an adoring look in her big eyes. If Mawgan noticed, he didn't let on, and that somehow made him an even better person.

They carried on strolling to the end of the path, back towards the palace, and as they rounded a corner, ran straight into King Branwalather.

'Ah, there you are,' growled Branwalather, his voice like gravel. Towering above them all, a mammoth of a man, he had looked big on the horse, but now he looked even bigger. His hair was white and thick, his face covered in worry lines. He stared at them all with his icy blue eyes. Tara wondered what he was thinking as he showed no emotion. He focussed his attention now on Niamh.

'Well, Mawgan,' he said. 'Are you going to introduce me to your friends?'

'Yes, my apologies, Uncle,' replied Mawgan. 'This is Jared and his sister Lucy. And this is Tara and her sister Niamh.'

After giving Jared and Lucy a cursory glance, Branwalather looked hard at Tara and Niamh. 'Sisters eh, is that right? How did human children come to be wandering this realm? And one of them have a realm child as a sister. Something peculiar is afoot I fear.'

He was frowning at Niamh as if trying to figure it all out, when one of his guards ran to him with a message.

'Excuse me one moment,' he said gruffly.

Branwalather stepped aside and unrolled the piece of parchment he'd been handed. His thick white brows knitted together.

'I will be along directly. Prepare the company for imminent departure.' He gave the order to the nearest guard. He turned to Mawgan. 'You must come with me. Princess Gwyn must sign the papers forthwith.'

Branwalather bowed in their direction by way of goodbye and walked away. Mawgan shrugged his shoulders in apology and followed. Tara's heart sank; this meant he wouldn't be coming with them. Something had obviously happened that called for their return to Dumnonia. The others looked at each other and they tagged on behind in the hope of learning more.

In the palace, there was a flurry of activity. People dashed here and there. Several official looking people appeared looking flustered. They hurried towards large double doors opening them wide. Tara could see Mawgan inside, he caught her eye, but two people closed the doors again.

Zira came and told them the reception would now wind down and she would serve them supper before bed.

Tara could see the others felt as dejected as she did. They ate in silence. They were on their own again.

Tara woke to find a set of warm clothes neatly laid out on a chair. Well, at least she wouldn't have to travel in the chilly weather in clothes meant for the indoors. They smelt like lavender. There was a warm blue cloak, and a long, blue-green gown that although made of wool, was as light as silk. At the bottom of the pile, she found her own scarf, still in one piece. She dressed, the gown fitted her like a glove and she felt so grown up. A pair of black boots finished off the ensemble. In a way, she'd be sorry to go back to her normal clothes.

Zira came in with her breakfast and to tell her Princess Gwyn would provide, with pleasure, anything they might need for the journey. Tara requested food and drink. Zira also asked if any of them could ride and Tara told her none of them could.

Zira reached into her pocket and handed Tara a note. 'This was given to me by Prince Mawgan's personal escort.'

Tara quickly broke the red seal and opened it. It read:

Greetings Tara,
Please not to worry, I will catch you up.
Until then I bid you farewell.
Your friend,
Mawgan, Prince of Dumnonia.

Tara spirits lifted. He would come with them after all. They had a friend to help them now, someone older and who knew the ways of the fae folk. She put on her boots with great enthusiasm.

A few minutes later Jared came to her room wearing his own clothes. He also had new boots.

'These are better to kick grislics with,' he said, grinning.

'Are the others ready?' she asked. Although she wanted to go on with the journey, she would miss the safety and friendliness of the palace.

'Yep, they've gone down already.'

'Okay then, let's go.'

Tara took her time walking down. At the bottom of the stairs, they found quite a gathering. Niamh and Lucy stood next to Princess Gwyn. Lucy wore new, warm clothing, similar to her own, though in shades of rust and brown. Her dress only reached her ankles. Tara's dress was longer – she appreciated Princess Gwyn treating her like an adult.

Guido, Udell, Avery and Sibéal made up the rest of the

farewell party, as did Zalen. Tara was surprised to find she was happy to see Zalen; she was beginning to think she would never see him again. When she said hello to him, he mumbled an answer and looked down at his feet. He didn't seem at all happy.

They all said their goodbyes and Zira handed over colourful backpacks to each of them, presumably holding food.

'You will find everything you require for your journey in the packs,' said Sibéal with a twinkle in her eye. 'Including one or two extra items of clothing.'

Tara remembered she and Lucy had arrived wet. She grinned.

Avery smiled reassuringly. 'Zalen is to go with you to show you the way. He was delighted to volunteer, were you not, Zalen?'

'Of course.' Zalen vigorously nodded his head. But he looked far from delighted to be going, Tara began to think he had been forced into it somehow. If Marvaanagh was trying to kill him, it wasn't surprising he didn't want to go back.

Princess Gwyn looked concerned. 'You could do with a friend out there. Although Zalen cannot help much, he will do what he can I am sure, and will advise you. It is a shame none of you ride or we could have loaned you some horses.'

Tears came into Tara's eyes. Everyone was so kind. She thanked them all enthusiastically. Princess Gwyn kissed Niamh first, also giving her a hug. She kissed Tara on both cheeks and then Lucy. Tara couldn't help thinking how much Donella must love having the princess as a relative.

Chapter Fifteen

The weather was crisp and cool, the early morning sun shone through the trees and the tips of the bracken glistened. It was deathly quiet except for the drip, drip, drip, as the frost melted off the trees.

An animal howled in the distance and it echoed through the silence, reminding Tara of the dangers of the forest. Her mouth was dry with fear. They didn't know what lay ahead. Who was this person Humbert? Princess Gwyn said he was a Jotunn. Tara hoped Jotunns were kind people. The Mordanta sounded sinister too, if they ever reached them that was. First, they had the ley tunnel to tackle, still Tara's greatest fear – well, only one of them, as she didn't fancy meeting the hare again or facing Queen Marvaanagh.

After about an hour, Zalen led them down a narrow path, which eventually widened onto a road. The trees began to thin and soon they came out of the forest. Tara could at last let her tense muscles relax; she hated being in the forest, with its many places for people and creatures – hares and dryads especially – to hide.

They walked on without stopping for at least another hour before Lucy asked could they rest for a while. Stopping by a large meadow filled with rocks they each found one to sit on.

They opened their bags and discovered an assortment of lovely food and drink packed away in them. Tara took a drink from the flask, only to find it the sweetest water she had ever tasted. She didn't know what nectar tasted like, but decided it must be just like this. She chose a ripe pear to eat, deciding to save the bread and cheese for later.

'Someone needs to keep a watch on the path,' said Tara, after eating her pear, 'in case Mawgan comes along, so I'll do it.' She walked back to the pathway and found a rock to sit on.

After quite some time she saw no sign of anyone on the road, disappointed, Tara was just thinking it was time to move on when she realised something was wrong. The ground began to tremble slightly and the vibrations rippled under her through the rock. She leapt up. The trembling worsened. Tara could hear rumbling as her rock began to move. To her dismay, other large rocks in the meadow began to move, then to roll. She cupped her hands around her mouth and yelled a warning to the others who were gathering their things in the middle of the meadow.

'Look out!' she shouted. They realised the urgency too late. 'Run!' she screamed.

'Hurry!' yelled Lucy, who was closest to Tara and reached her first. She pointed to the moving rocks.

'Run, run!' screamed Tara again, jumping up and down with frustration.

The rocks began to lift off the ground, flying through the air, each one landing at quite a distance away. It was as if invisible giants were picking them up and throwing them, thought Tara, panic rising. One landed right in front of a startled Niamh, who screeched and jumped out of the way. Without looking back, they all ran like mad.

A rock landed close to Tara and Lucy. Tara grabbed Lucy and pulled her away from the meadow. Crashing thuds boomed behind them as the rocks hit the ground.

Once on the safety of the path Tara swung around. 'Look out to the left!' she screamed as a rock headed towards Zalen. Tara's heart skipped a beat; he would never get out of the way in time.

Niamh spotted the rock, she stared up at it and it slowed in the air just enough for Jared to pull Zalen sideways. It fell to the ground with a sickening thud. Tara let out a long breath as with a mixture of cursing and yelling, they all joined her and Lucy in the road.

'Thank you Jared for pushing me out of the way,' Zalen gasped. 'Throwing rocks is usually my domain, not having them thrown at me.'

Jared nodded at him and said matter-of-factly, 'I think Queen Mar-watsit had something to do with this!'

'Marvaanagh,' said Tara. 'Niamh, I don't know what you did there, but you saved Zalen, not Jared.'

'Yes, erm thank you, thank you very much,' said Zalen. 'I did not realise you had managed to do this, Niamh.' Tara appreciated he hadn't known Niamh had somehow used her new magical ability to slow the rock down, but then neither did Jared. 'And yes, Jared helped by pushing you out of the way,' she conceded.

Niamh looking puzzled. 'I don't know how I did it either. I wish I did, that would be brilliant!'

Lucy stared at Niamh in awe and Tara had to smile, but she was actually feeling in awe herself, no time to think on that now though. 'How far is it to Rath Sarog, Zalen,' she asked, worried they would be attacked again.

'Not more than an hour I should think,' he replied. 'As long as we do not encounter any problems along the way. We should leave the road and walk alongside the river.'

'We can't. Mawgan said he would catch us up and he'll come along the road, I'm sure,' said Tara. Just then, they heard the sounds of hooves and someone came galloping around the corner on a shiny black stallion. The animal looked magnificent in a black leather bridle studded with brass ornaments. It took Tara a moment to realise it was Mawgan, as he no longer wore the resplendent clothes she had last seen him in. He reined in when he saw them and dismounted.

'I thought I would never catch you up. Truly, it was not as easy to escape my duties as I thought. I have the betrothal papers.' He patted his chest where the scroll protruded from inside his plain brown tunic. 'These are my excuse for coming with you. To deliver them to Queen Marvaanagh, I also told my uncle I would try to find out what was going on, for surely he had noticed something was amiss. So he reluctantly agreed.'

'Why did you have to leave so suddenly,' asked Niamh.

'There has been a Kawpangian raid on Dumnonia. My uncle had to return immediately. The attacks happen all the time. The Kawpangian Jotunns can land anywhere along the coast. They seem to navigate the dangerous waters without too much problem. They come across the sea, from a land far to the north.'

Tara gulped. 'Jotunns! Humbert is a Jotunn!'

'Do not be distressed, he is not of the same tribe. His tribe are giant trolls. The Kawpangian Jotunns are about my size and from much further north and are led by Skalle. He killed my aunt and my parents.'

'Oh I'm sorry to hear that,' said Tara with as much sympathy as she could muster. 'There's so much danger everywhere.'

'Yes, and here in Wiltunscire too I am afraid,' agreed Mawgan.

'We need to make sure we stick close together,' said Niamh, furtively looking around. 'Zalen thinks we should travel the rest of the way off the main route.'

'I don't want to go near the river,' whimpered Lucy. 'Say it gets all wild again?'

'It is for the best, Lucy,' said Mawgan kindly. 'Do not worry, I doubt Marvaanagh will try the same trick twice. Let us not tarry.' And with that he put his hands on Lucy's shoulders and directed her forwards.

Lucy coloured up, but smiled, and running up to Niamh, linked arms with her.

Mawgan took the reins of his horse.

They soon reached the river, which was smooth as a lake. Nothing remained of the raging turbulence of two days before, not even a scrap of debris. Swans, geese and ducks, swam happily about, bobbing under the water every so often for titbits to eat. If it did rain, they could always move away and back onto the main roadway, decided Tara.

As they walked along the narrow path, Mawgan told them a

little about his life and explained how he had known Princess Donella since he was just a little boy. He told them how they had played together during the few times they had met. When they grew up, King Branwalather and Queen Marvaanagh had encouraged their betrothal. He and his uncle both felt they couldn't refuse for the sake of the realms, especially after what happened to Queen Anya and King Edmwnd. His uncle needed help from the other realms to fight the Kawpangians. It was purely coincidental Mawgan and Donella had come to care for one another. He now knew of course it wasn't so simple and something more sinister skulked behind Marvaanagh's eagerness. It obviously wasn't because she wanted to rally the folk of the realms to help Dumnonia.

Tara wondered what Mawgan really thought about being pressed into marrying someone at so young an age, she thought he was perhaps eighteen or nineteen, but on the surface, he seemed to accept it.

After travelling for a good while, they came to a small field with a scarecrow in the middle and Tara suggested it a good place to stop so Mawgan could eat something.

Tara unwound her scarf and taking off her cloak, laid it on the ground, and sat down on it. 'Ah, look at that,' she said, pointing to the scarecrow. 'Poor thing, he's so bedraggled.'

'W-what?' asked Mawgan, following her direction. 'Ah, you mean the galley-bagger.'

'We call it a scarecrow,' said Tara. Her eyes kept drifting to the scarecrow, badly dressed in only a tatty shirt and ragged trousers. His turnip head was bare. 'Poor thing,' she said again.

'You're a softy, Tara.' Niamh grinned. 'It's only a scarecrow, erm, galley-bagger.'

While Mawgan ate, everyone recounted their experiences with the flying rocks. Tara thought how anyone passing by would think they were just having a picnic on a pleasant autumn day in the countryside, with the sun shining and birds singing, not knowing the dangers they actually faced around every corner and that they had to be constantly vigilant.

Tara couldn't take her focus off the galley-bagger and not being able to help herself, took her scarf to it and tied it around his neck. Mum wouldn't mind knitting another for her. Stepping back and surveying him, she gave a grunt of satisfaction and sauntered back to the others just as Zalen began to lead the horse back from the river.

Once Mawgan had finished eating, they continued on their way.

Jared walked along to Mawgan's horse. With a sweep of his arms, he appeared to scoop up something from the ground. His arms came back up as if to place something on the saddle.

'There you go then, Leanne,' he said to the invisible figure on the horse. 'Now it's easier to keep up with us.'

Tara blushed at the embarrassment of it. Mawgan smiled at him as if Jared was being very thoughtful.

It grew colder and Tara put on her cloak.

'You're going to get cold, Tara, without your scarf, once the sun goes in,' said Niamh.

'Has she lost it?' asked Mawgan.

'No, she put it on the scarecrow.'

'What!' cried Zalen. 'Surely not, oh no!'

'Oh yes, I did,' said Tara wondering what all the fuss was about. 'I felt sorry for it.'

Zalen turned and ran back up the river path. Icy fingers played with Tara's heart, she ran after him, nausea rising in her throat. What could be the matter? What had she done? She caught up with him standing on the edge of the field, despair in his eyes. The scarf had vanished.

'Where's it gone?' asked Tara, searching around to see if she could see it. 'Someone's stolen it.'

'Unfortunately,' said Zalen gravely. 'You should never put your own clothes on a galley-bagger; someone can take them and use them in magic against you. And it may be that they...well most likely Queen Marvaanagh or one of her cronies, has done just that.'

Tara put her hands over her face; she thought she would be sick. 'Oh, I didn't know!' she cried. 'Honestly, I didn't know.'

Mawgan had caught up with them. 'It was not your fault. We should have warned you. It is something we take for granted here. I would think that most likely it has had a bewitchment placed on it and that is why you were attracted towards it.'

Feeling a little better, Tara took her hands from her face and they trudged back to the others to tell them.

'What will happen now?' asked Niamh.

'We have to hope it is someone who has taken a fancy to its bright colour,' said Mawgan desolately. 'But if it is Queen Marvaanagh...and it is rather a coincidence, well, she can use it in magic to hurt Tara as she now owns something personal of hers.'

Subdued they continued on their way. Tara, her head bent, studied the ground. She could only hope Marvaanagh didn't have her scarf; she couldn't bear to think what she might do with it. How could such a simple gesture go so wrong? Had Marvaanagh indeed planned it that way, planned to single her out?

Tara thought back to the incident with the bridge. Marvaanagh had targeted her...and Lucy. She would probably guess Tara wouldn't be aware of the consequences and planted the galley-bagger in the field. It must be Marvaanagh's doing. Harvest was well over, so a scarecrow wasn't needed. She sighed, why worry about it now...it had happened, she must stay constantly on her guard, and not trust anything.

Lucy put her arm around her. 'Don't worry. You've got us lot to look after you.'

Niamh, who was walking in front of her wrapping her scarf around her neck, turned and smiled her reassurance, drawing

Tara's eyes to the long fringe. Her own scarf had the longer fringe. Niamh was wearing *her* scarf! Tara grabbed hold of it and stared at it in dismay. They must have somehow got them mixed up. Niamh's scarf, not her own…was on the galley-bagger. Tara couldn't believe it. Niamh stared quizzically at her and eventually it dawned on her too.

'I'm so sorry, Niamh, really, really sorry.'

There was what seemed to Tara a long pause before Niamh said brightly, 'That's okay, she can't hurt me. I have the bracelet protecting me…see.' She held her wrist out and Tara felt a little better. 'You don't have anything to protect you. So it's all for the best.'

Tara gave her a weak smile and hugged her. How could Niamh be so reasonable about it? She saw a signpost over Niamh's shoulder. Pointing to it, she hurried over to examine it. It gave her the opportunity to fight away her tears.

Forgetting her misery in an instant, she exclaimed in surprise, 'We're going the wrong way! The signpost clearly says Rath Sarog is in the opposite direction.'

The others swiftly joined her.

'How can that be?' cried Niamh.

'Maybe we passed it already,' said Lucy.

Mawgan stiffened. 'Someone is tricking us. We could not have passed it. It is an enormous timber castle with outer ditches. And it cannot be the other way as it is further down in the valley not further up.'

He reached up and swung the sign around. Now it said Vrogoly Forest and pointed back the way they had come. Tara trudged around to the other side and Rath Sarog now pointed down to the valley.

'Hmm, maybe there is a duergar around,' said Mawgan.

'What's one of those?' asked Lucy, her eyes as big as saucers.

'They guard the paths and try to stop folk from reaching certain places.'

'Do you mean it's been sent by someone, Queen Marvaanagh maybe? I mean...to stop us from getting to Rath Sarog?' asked Niamh.

'We cannot be sure,' replied Mawgan, 'as they often do this on the pathways.' He paused, rubbing his chin. 'However, I do not think we should be too concerned unless we run into him again.'

'Say we do though, I've had enough of problems,' said Tara. She was weary of all this. She just wanted the whole thing over with so they could all go home. Somehow, it had all lost its excitement. It wasn't just her. She could see everyone was tired.

Mawgan came along side of her. 'Do not be too concerned, Tara,' he said. 'It will be all right.'

'Yes, you worry too much about everything, Tara,' agreed Niamh. 'It's probably nothing.'

'Yeah, when I think about it, you do go on a bit,' Jared added.

'Oh thanks, everyone. You just don't see that we have to be wary of everything...*everything*!' But she directed her glare at Jared, how dare he!

'Duergars are not that dangerous, just a bit tricky,' said Mawgan.

Tara let him carry on thinking her worries concerned the duergar. She didn't want him to know she was angry, mostly with herself, for allowing them to get into all this in the first place. She had willingly come along even encouraged it, without a thought of what could happen if they passed through the gateway, and now they faced constant danger. So, wasn't it her duty to look after them all...to ensure they got home safely? They could tease her all they wanted, she wouldn't stop watching out for them.

Having resigned herself to her fate, she took a deep breath and stepped up the pace, holding her head high.

As Tara turned a corner, she almost ran into a fallen tree, which stretched across the path, blocking it. She immediately sought a way around the branches. Thinking it might be easier to go around the trunk end where it had snapped off, she pushed her way through the hedgerow and into a field.

'Hey there, are you not going to help me?' shouted a voice.

Tara halted in her tracks and seeing the others still remained on the other side, she pushed her way back through the hedgerow and found herself standing behind Jared. Mawgan scrabbled around among the golden leaves. He suddenly stood up.

'What's up?' asked Jared. 'What is it?'

Chapter Sixteen

A deep frown wrinkled Mawgan's forehead. 'Perhaps you should see this for yourself.'

They all stepped forward, but Tara had a problem seeing anything.

'Ahhh,' said Lucy.

'Who are you?' asked Niamh.

By pushing through some leafy branches and scratching herself into the bargain, at last Tara could see to whom it was Niamh spoke. Trapped under a branch lying in a puddle was a tiny, broad set, dwarf-like man. His face was dark and wizened; he wore a green hat, which lay skew-whiff, and a miniature sheepskin jacket.

'We need to get him out!' she said, and couldn't understand why Mawgan had stepped back.

'Are you hurt?' she asked the dwarf-like creature.

'My name is Braedon, I have hurt my leg,' he replied.

Tara felt a hand on her shoulder. 'Come away for a moment, I must to speak to you all,' whispered Mawgan.

Tara hesitated and Mawgan nodded to her. Reluctantly she turned away, followed by the others.

'What is it, Mawgan?' asked Jared.

'He is a duergar. Probably the one who is trying to confuse us with the road sign.'

'But he's hurt,' protested Tara. 'He needs our help.'

'Duergars cannot be trusted. They are also strong creatures and he should have no problem getting out of there. This could be a trap. It could be he was indeed sent here – by Queen Marvaanagh even, as Niamh said earlier.'

'But we can't just leave him!' cried Tara.

'I vote we leave him,' demanded Jared. 'Leanne does too. I think we should listen to her.'

Tara threw him one of her withering looks. 'That's just the sort of thing I would expect you to say,' she snapped. 'I wouldn't leave an injured rat here, never mind a – a little man! And anyway, who's worried now!'

'Not worried...just cautious,' Jared snapped back.

'I'm not sure about this, Tara,' said Niamh. 'I have a bad feeling.'

'I think we should help him,' decided Lucy.

'Pleeease help me,' called Braedon, his voice feeble. 'My leg hurts.'

'Okay,' said Niamh.

Tara's eyes questioned Mawgan and Jared.

'Well, on your own heads be it,' declared Jared.

'I am not sure about this, yet I will do it,' said Mawgan moving forward.

Mawgan and Jared dragged the branches aside to free him. What was the matter with them all? A minute ago, they said she was too cautious and now she was being the opposite they didn't like that either. She couldn't do anything right. Tara helped lift the last few small twigs away from Braedon.

'Watch out!' he cried. 'You are hurting me.'

They lifted him out and stared down at him, lying on the path at their feet.

'So now we have him out, what next?' asked Jared.

Tara hadn't thought of that. But she wasn't going to let Jared know it. 'Where do you live? We can take you home. Or fetch someone for you.'

'I live far away. Take me to Humbert...he will help. He will heal.'

'That would be Rath Sarog,' said Mawgan, his frown deepening.

Braedon groaned as if badly hurt. 'Just a wee way down the path it is.'

Mawgan sighed. 'All right, I will put him on my horse.'

'Wait!' cried Braedon. 'Find my music first!'

'Music?' said Mawgan.

'Lucy scrabbled around in the branches. 'I think he means this.' She pulled out a small, ornate musical instrument rather like a miniature harp, but with only three strings.

'Now get a move on! And be sure to hold me on. I hate horses!' moaned Braedon.

My goodness, how rude and ungrateful he was, thought Tara, as Mawgan lifted him from the ground. Still, Tara could see Mawgan wasn't happy about doing it. How much of a problem could he be? Jared took Leanne off the horse and Mawgan put Braedon on. Lucy kept hold of the harp.

'Give me my music,' demanded Braedon.

'You're very rude. I wasn't going to hurt it,' snapped Lucy, and roughly slammed it down on top of him.

Not far around the corner, Rath Sarog appeared through the trees, and was not quite what Tara had expected. Set a hundred or so metres off the path, the wooden castle stood on a grass covered earth mound, which in turn sat on another smaller earth mound, built up in layers, rather like a wedding cake, with a huge base. A home for a giant – she began to get cold feet. She boldly turned towards it, her stomach churning.

Braedon began to wriggle, fear etched on his shrivelled face.

'Keep still, Duergar, you are annoying my horse,' snapped Mawgan. 'And if you do not stop, you can walk in.'

A wooden bridge stretched uphill across an enormous ditch. They walked uneasily across it on to the top of the first flat layer of the base of the great mound. It was quite a trek across the grass on up to an immense wooden drawbridge, which led to the second smaller mound and the castle. Tara hoped Humbert wouldn't suddenly pull it up, leaving them stranded.

'Keep still, I said, Duergar,' snapped Mawgan again, obviously still having problems with Braedon. The wooden slatted bridge was not easy for a horse to negotiate so Braedon had a rough ride. It wasn't just that though, for as the castle loomed nearer, the more fearful Braedon became. Tara couldn't understand his reluctance. If he knew Humbert, why be afraid of him?

'Here, let me carry him, perhaps we should leave the horse here,' said Jared, and Mawgan gladly pulled Braedon off and handed him over. Jared looked down at Leanne as if it were the most natural thing in the world to be talking to her. 'Don't worry, Leanne. I'm not afraid of him. Maybe Tara can hold your hand for a bit.'

'Don't be stupid, Jared,' snarled Tara.' She moved ahead to walk with Mawgan. Did Jared really think she was going to walk along holding hands with nothing?

The castle rose up in front of them. They stepped onto the drawbridge and slowly edged their way along it. A great door with an even greater knocker greeted them on the other side. This wasn't a good idea. Tara's usual tinkling niggles clanged more like alarm bells. If they went in, something bad would happen. The portentous feeling overwhelmed her.

Mawgan took the knocker in both hands and banged as hard as he could. A crashing sound came from within the castle and the loud thudding of the giants footsteps brought him to the door. It creaked open and Tara jumped back in surprise from the ugly, giant man, of at least four metres high, who glared down at them. Dressed in a linen shirt with wide sleeves, leather waistcoat and knee length trousers, his hairy lower legs and feet bare, he wore a number of gold arms bands and bangles. His hair was in need of a good combing.

Humbert looked taken aback when he spotted Braedon. 'What do you bring to my door, elf?'

'Humbert the Jotunn,' said Mawgan. 'We most humbly beg your pardon. Princess Gwyn asked us to visit you. On the way, we found this duergar injured by a tree. He asked us to bring him here, so you can heal him.'

Humbert scowled, opening the door wide to reveal a small courtyard.

'The duergar stays here. The rest of you...friends of Princess Gwyn...can enter my home.'

Jared put Braedon down on a bench. Humbert stooped over him and rubbing his hands together paused before placing them on the leg indicated to him by Braedon. After two minutes, Humbert stood back.

'You have a short time to rest and then you leave,' boomed Humbert his great arm pointing to the open door.

'Come in, friends,' Humbert said to the rest of them lowering his voice as he spoke. And with his head bowed and his shoulders hunched, he led the way inside the castle.

Tara looked guiltily back to where Braedon lay. He scowled petulantly. 'I do not care. I have my music,' he said, throwing her a malevolent look. Turning to the instrument he angrily began to pluck at the strings making a far from musical sound.

What an ungrateful wretch, Tara turned, refusing to feel sorry for him any longer. She trailed behind the others into a small hall, which had several doors leading off. One of the doors stood open and led into a bigger hall.

Braedon was soon far from her thoughts, as she looked around surprised at how comfortable the castle looked with its armchairs, tables, heavy purple velvet curtains, and brightly woven rugs covering the rough wooden floor. She moved over to the fire in the centre of the room, the enormous brick chimney above it reaching high up into the eaves. Warming her hands, she laughed for the first time in what seemed like an age, when she saw Niamh and Lucy trying to scramble onto one of the giant sized armchairs.

She glanced around, somewhere here there must be a gateway, and shortly they would have to broach the subject. At the thought of the ley tunnel, her stomach did a somersault. The sooner it was over with the better. Princess Gwyn had said the purer the purpose the safer it became to travel the ley. Tara decided it depended on which way you looked at it. They needed help to get into a castle. A castle they would be breaking into. That wasn't exactly pure. Of course, they would be doing it for a good reason. Queen Marvaanagh wanted to kill them. They had to stop her and set free Princess Donella, a virtual prisoner at Caer Searesby. There it was then, a pure enough purpose, of that she was certain.

'It is good to have visitors,' said Humbert, a grin breaking out over his ugly features, showing more than one missing tooth. 'You like to play *boules* with me? Or you like to eat something? I have pigeon left over from lunch.'

'Erm, a game of *boules* sounds very nice,' said Niamh hastily. She whispered to Tara, 'We'd better play. We don't know if it's safe to eat here, even though I'm a bit hungry.' This astounded Tara, not that she thought it safe to eat or not, but that she could even think of eating pigeon. Still, at least Niamh had remembered to be careful about eating food.

'Do you think it would be all right if Tara and Jared used the gateway for a short while,' asked Niamh. 'While we play *boules* with you.'

'The gateway? Why, do you need to use the ley?' asked Humbert.

Tara looked at Mawgan who nodded to her. 'We need to go to Caer Sidi to visit the Mordanta.' That's all she could think of to say, but it seemed to be enough.

'All right, but when you come back there is a fee to be paid.'

Tara didn't know what to say, this must be the fee Princess Gwyn talked about. What did they need to give him? They didn't have anything of value she could think of. Perhaps they should worry about that when they came back.

Humbert had turned and walked away indicating for them to follow.

Zalen ran behind them. 'Enter the gateway and the ley will

carry you along feet first. Eventually, a blue light will illuminate the tunnel and you will emerge at the great stone circle. Look to the north, there should be no trouble spotting a lone, tall tower, this is Caer Sidi. You will find the Mordanta there. Return the same way.'

'What do we do about paying Humbert,' asked Tara.

Zalen shrugged. 'We will figure that out when you come back. It will probably be some small token.'

Humbert led them to the back of the building. A wooden archway awkwardly tucked away in a corner, led to nowhere.

'That is the gateway,' said Humbert pointing to it. 'Good journey be with you.'

'Thank you, Humbert,' said Tara.

'Thanks,' echoed Jared.

They looked at each other and walked towards it. Tara turned to give Niamh her cloak, thinking it might hamper her, before stepping forward to stand next to Jared in front of the archway.

'Do you want me to go first,' asked Jared. He turned around and told Leanne to stay and wait for him.

'Er...yes, okay,' replied Tara. She didn't want Jared to know she felt afraid, terrified even, to make the first step through.

Zalen said again, 'Now remember to just let it take you. Keep your arms crossed over your chest and your legs tucked in until you see the blue light.'

Jared turned around and grinned, stepping through, he promptly vanished. Tara stood staring at the empty corner, trying not to think about what was happening to Jared. Her feet took root.

Chapter Seventeen

'Do you want me to go instead?' offered Niamh, as Tara stood like a statue, not daring to move.

Tara shook her head, not just to say no, but also in an attempt to bring herself to her senses. Crossing her arms across her chest, she stepped in.

Without warning, Tara found her breath torn from her lungs, her feet whisked from beneath her. Twirling her around, the ley pulled her into a horizontal position and hurtled her down the tunnel.

She screamed. At first her arms flailed as she lost control. Scraping her hand on something, she quickly pulled her arms back in. She had never felt so frightened. The ley closed in on her and she could see nothing in the pitch-blackness. Tara found it hard to breathe, the cold air seeming to freeze her lungs. It was like sliding down a huge slide, but in mid-air, a horrible sensation of falling.

Every so often, she would twist around and around, making her head spin. She kept looking for the blue light, hoping it would all be over with in a trice, she saw nothing. There was no indication of how long she would continue to be tortured. Things grazed her hair and face, like spider webs, which she wanted to brush away, but didn't dare move her arms. Helpless, she had no choice but to accept it and wait for it all to end.

At last, after travelling what felt like miles at speed, the blue light lit up the ley tunnel. Tara could see tree roots sticking out everywhere and bits of rock and stone, only by a miracle did she not hit anything. A few seconds later, she found herself hanging upside down before landing with a bump on the ground.

'Ouch!' she cried.

She was lying on grass, flat on her back. Jared loomed over her. She had a strange feeling of déjà vu.

'You okay? Some ride! Like being on the scariest rollercoaster ever.' He sat down on the grass next to her.

'Er, yeah,' she lied. 'I'm fine, great fun.' Actually, she felt like throwing up and the scratch on her hand stung. Rubbing it, she sat up and looked around.

'Oh my gosh! It's Stonehenge!' she gasped.

'Well, it looks like it, but it's kinda different.'

Yes, different, Tara could see straight away, a perfect circle of huge stones bridged with lintel stones. Tara and Jared were sitting right in the middle of an inner circle of large stones facing what she identified, from her visits with Uncle Fergus, as the altar stone. Tara turned, two huge stones rose up behind them with a lintel on top. This, she decided, must be the gateway. Well at least they knew how to get back into the ley.

The world had stopped spinning so Tara stood up. 'We need to find Caer Sidi. We should be able to see it from here.' Her curiosity about the Mordanta was growing fast. Who were they and why would they be willing to help? In fact, she wondered, what they would be able to do to help them. It would be wonderful if, by some magic, they could get back to Rath Sarog without having to travel the ley again.

Jared walked to the edge of the stone circle and turned slowly around until he directly faced the sun. He turned on his heel facing in the opposite direction, pointing. 'That's about north. I can see it, it's just over there.'

Tara ran over to him. The tower stood on a slope a couple of hundred metres away. They ambled towards it hesitatingly, not quite as eager as before, now they could see it.

When they reached the oak door, studded with nails and reinforced with bands of iron, they found no knocker, not even a bell. Jared pushed the door and it opened.

'Anybody there,' he called. He grimaced at Tara.

'Enter children and be welcome.' The voice echoed around the building. It was an old cackling voice, like the witch in Hansel and Gretel. Uncle Fergus had told them the story when she and Niamh were little girls. He would imitate the cackling voice, and Tara would have nightmares about it.

'Ascend the stairway,' cackled the voice again, and the goose bumps sprang up on Tara's arms.

Stone steps stretched upwards, cold and forbidding. Not being able to see far in the darkness, Jared took a bright lamp from a windowsill.

'I'll go first,' he said. The stairs spiralled upwards and Tara's legs ached by the time they reached a heavy iron door at the top.

Jared placed the lamp on the floor, as the light from a small window lit the landing. He banged on the door once with the rusty old knocker. The door creaked open all by itself.

'Enter,' croaked the same voice they had heard on entering the tower.

They hesitantly inched their way through the door, into a sparsely furnished circular room. Three extraordinary women stood or sat around a half-finished colourful tapestry, stretched on a large wooden loom. Fire torches threw gigantic sinister shadows on the walls. Apart from a long wooden bench placed along one wall, three rocking chairs were positioned around a small fireplace.

The youngest woman turned and smiled at them. She sat at the loom, wearing a white brocade gown, her long red hair trailing the floor. She didn't pause in her task, dexterously working a bobbin back and forth over the warp.

'I am Zoey,' she said. 'Welcome.'

The second, more sinister, witch, stood to the right of the loom holding a pair of large and ancient scissors, whose pointed blades glistened. Over her face and most of her body, hung a long white veil.

'I am Zofia,' she whispered, nodding her head in greeting.

The third woman, an old crone dressed in black, with scraggly white hair, a hooked nose and crooked back, stood to the left of the loom and held a spool of white thread in her hands.

'I am Zihna,' she croaked, and Tara recognised her voice as the one who had asked them to enter. 'Who is it that disturbs the peace of the Mordanta?'

Two of the witches had identical yellow-green eyes. Tara couldn't see the eyes of the third. When the eyes of one witch moved, the eyes of the other seemed to move spookily in unison. Tara spoke up, as Jared seemed dumbstruck. 'I'm Tara and this is my friend Jared.'

The crone Zihna, moved closer to Tara, so close her acrid breath wafted onto her face. Tara stood frozen to the spot as Zihna examined her closely.

'Well now...Tara...I see,' said Zihna. 'Hmm, you have come for help, I believe.'

'Yes,' said Tara. 'Princess Gwyn said you might be able to assist us. We need help to protect us from Queen Marvaanagh at Caer Searesby. She's trying to kill us. We wouldn't go there, but we must speak with Donella, she might need help too as she could also be in danger. In fact many of us are in danger...apparently.' It all came out in one go, and even to Tara it sounded ridiculous.

Zihna looked deep into Tara's eyes. 'We shall provide aid, Tara,' croaked Zihna. 'But heed our advice – whatever we provide you with – it is Craebh Ciuil, the silver wand of the true Queen of Wiltunscire that you need to fight the magic of Marvaanagh.'

'Life is not easy here in this land,' added Zoey. 'And it will challenge you even more in the coming days. Be sure you are ready for it. Once you embark on this adventure, you will find it hard to break away from these realms. You will also find it difficult to go back to your old world as you once knew it.'

Tara shivered as if someone had trampled over her grave. The trio of witches moved to one side, huddling together in conference, they mumbled away for a few minutes before turning in unison.

Zihna waved her spool and it turned into a colourful tapestry drawstring bag with a belt on which to hang it.

'Come forth, Tara.' Zihna smiled encouragingly at her.

Tara didn't hesitate and stepped forward.

Zihna held the bag out to her. 'This is the Purse of Plenty, Tara.' she croaked. 'It is filled with gold. Use it wisely. Never undervalue the power it holds.'

Tara took the purse gazing at it wondrously. Before she had time to examine it, Zoey waved her shuttle and it turned into an ornate enamelled hand mirror. It had with it a colourful woven tapestry bag on a string. She held out the mirror and the bag.

'This is Scathantar,' she said. 'Whomsoever it reflects will cross over to another place. Use it wisely, as it will return to us once it is drawn upon three times.'

Tara went to her. Up close, she could see Zoey had skin like a porcelain doll, her copper red hair accentuating it. Yet her features were sharp and her nose pointed.

Tara took Scathantar, placed it into the bag being careful not to look in it, and put it over her head to hang safely over one shoulder. She stepped back thinking through all the possibilities a mirror, which transports people to other places, might have.

Zofia waved her scissors and they turned into an iron dagger. It had a strange ornate jagged section cut out of the middle of it. With it came a woven leather scabbard and belt.

'Come forth, warrior Jared,' whispered Zofia, as she stood ghostlike with the dagger held up threateningly.

Surprisingly, Jared the warrior was most reluctant and needed a push from Tara, who couldn't help smirking, before stepping forward. Zofia held out the dagger and scabbard.

'This is Swifan, Jared,' said Zofia, her veil waving eerily as she spoke. 'It protects against magic and is a useful tool. Use it wisely, do not lose it, you will find it crucial to solving problems.'

Jared took the dagger and placed it in the scabbard. He

fastened it around his waist. Tara could see his proud and wondrous expression, and as he stepped back, she glimpsed a different Jared than she had ever seen before.

'Go now from our presence,' said Zofia. 'You have yet a long way to travel.

And do not underestimate what you view as the weakest of the gifts,' rasped Zihna.

'We won't. Thank you,' gushed Tara. 'Thank you so much.'

Jared added his thanks too and they turned and left the room. As they stood at the top of the stairs, Tara heard a beating sound, which became louder and louder. She jumped with fright and Jared grabbed at her arm as a large raven flew in through the open window and settled on the ledge.

'For crying out loud!' cried Jared.

'I nearly had a heart attack,' gasped Tara. She shivered, it looked remarkably similar to the one she had seen at the mound.

'You're not the only one,' said Jared. 'Come on let's get out of here.' He picked up the lamp he had earlier left outside and they dashed down the winding stairs, using the cold walls as support, not stopping until they reached the bottom.

'Cripes, what d'you make of that then?' said Jared, trying to catch his breath as he replaced the lamp. He glanced back up the stairs to see if they were being followed. 'Creepy or what?'

Tara turned her attention to the purse and opened it. 'Look at this!' she squeaked, showing him the golden contents of the Purse of Plenty.

'Real gold, I bet.' Jared stared at it admiringly. 'Hey, Tara, why can't we use your mirror to take us to back to Rath Sarog. It would save us having to travel that ley again.'

Tara laughed, and it unravelled the tension out of her taut muscles. 'Because twit, Zoey didn't say it took people to a particular place, just another one, and that could be Dumnonia for all we know.'

'Oh yeah,' said Jared, grinning sheepishly. 'I was expecting a big shiny sword, what damage could this do?' He pulled out the dagger and holding it up, wiggled it.

'Remember what the Mordanta told us. It's a tool, which can help with problems and protects against magic. But what we actually need to find is Craebh Ciuil, the wand that can fight Marvaanagh's magic. Princess Gwyn said the same thing'

'Oh well, that's something. I suppose we'll have to wait to find out.'

With that, they made their way back to the Caer Sidi gateway.

Chapter Eighteen

Two hours had passed. Donella checked on her maid and hearing gentle snoring crept back along to the secret passageway. After lighting the lamp, she swiftly moved down the stairs. This time she brought the tinderbox with her. She blew out the lamp before going into the main part of the castle and stealthily managed to find her way to the north wing without being seen by any grislic guards. The moon lit her way for the most part, and for the rest of it, she felt her way along, keeping close to the wall.

Donella waited until she had entered her parents' room before lighting the lamp again. She looked around. What object could Marvaanagh have moved? Absent of personal belongings, it had a rug, a huge chest, two armchairs upholstered in sumptuous rich blue material and an elaborately carved chest of drawers. Family portraits hung on the wall.

Donella pulled open the chest to find it empty. She tried the drawers, but they were empty too.

One of the portraits caught her eye, as it was slightly askew. The painting depicted an image of one of the previous queens from many centuries before. Carefully lifting it down, which although not very big, was heavy, she immediately realised something lay behind it. She hurriedly put the portrait on the floor, leaning it against the wall.

Excited now, Donella saw a glass case set in the wall. In it, on purple velvet, lay a slim silver branch — Craebh Ciuil! Donella had known of the wand, it had belonged to her mother, passed down through the female line of the family. A gift given by the folk of the land of Iwernia across the sea, to the Queen of the Realm of Wiltunscire as a symbol of peace many centuries ago, it helped defend the realm from negative magic.

The wand enhanced magical abilities and bestowed new ones. Up until now, her aunt had led Donella to believe the wand was still with her mother on Ynys Is. She must have been trying to take it by magic, but only the true owner could remove it from the solid glass case and she was not the true owner, Donella herself was. Why had she lied?

Donella touched the glass – nothing happened. It should open. Somewhere in the back of her mind, she remembered the owner only had access to the wand if they were deemed mature enough to use it and in times of great need. Magic should not be used lightly. Perhaps she could only take it from the case after her marriage, for surely there was need enough, but perhaps not. She replaced the portrait and blowing out her lamp at the door, she took one last look at the chamber, which once belonged to her parents, and quietly closed the door.

As she sneaked back along the hallways and galleries, somewhere in the deep recesses of her mind, Donella could feel her mother's touch. Once she had a mother who had really loved her, cared for her, and had comforted her when she cried.

Thinking back over the years, she could think of no instance when Marvaanagh had taken her in her arms, loved her, kissed her, wiped away her tears. Yes, she had good food, clothing, and as a child she had maids to see to her every need, though they had been dismissed as soon as she was able to dress herself. But never had she felt a mother's love from Marvaanagh, only from her Aunt Gwyn, once or twice a year, during her stays.

Of course, she had her memories – memories she could not quite grasp and bring forth into her conscious mind, because she was so very young when she lost her parents.

A time for change was coming – she could feel it. A better time she hoped, filled with love, real caring and a sense of family life she had never had.

Donella had almost reached the buttery when two figures jumped out on her from the bottom of the stairwell. Her breath caught in her throat threatening to choke her. Alarmed, she dropped her lamp and it made a resounding clank as she backed up against the wall. Gruesome grislic goblins – she recognised them as Dargen and Grud.

'Ahh, now what have we here? A little princess no less,' sneered Dargen, not even bothering to conceal his glee.

Grud sneered malevolently and Donella flinched. 'We saw through the window someone creeping about in the corridor. What will your aunt have to say about this?'

They laughed and grabbing her arms dragged her off towards the great chamber.

* * *

Arriving back at Rath Sarog with a bump, Tara was relieved to find the journey back along the ley wasn't quite as terrifying as the journey there. Likely because she knew what to expect, and this time kept her arms tight in from the start.

They found the others had finished their game of boules and now sat around a table in Humbert's kitchen. Niamh handed Tara her cloak, which she was thankful to put on, as it had been cold in the ley tunnel.

'Now you pay me for using the gateway,' said Humbert on seeing them. 'Everyone has to pay.'

'What can we give you,' asked Mawgan as Tara was lost for words.

'What gifts did the Mordanta give to you?' Humbert directed this at Jared.

'Erm…a dagger, a purse and a mirror.'

'You choose, but you must give me one of these gifts,' Humbert insisted. 'Everyone has to pay.'

Tara and Jared gathered everyone around and explained the gifts. 'We have to give him what we think is the least useful,' said Tara.

'Indeed,' answered Mawgan. 'But knowing the Mordanta, all these items are useful and important.'

'How about the dagger?' offered Jared. 'It doesn't look as if it could cut anything.'

'It protects against magic,' said Tara. 'So I think we need it. What about the mirror?'

Mawgan tapped his chin with the tips of his fingers. 'The mirror may get us out of danger as it can transport anyone who looks deeply into it, to another place.'

'What about the gold in the purse? We don't have to give it all to him, and anyway, what good can it do us?' Niamh held out the Purse of Plenty.

Tara nodded. 'Yes, I think it's the least useful.'

They all looked at each other and mumbled agreement. Tara opened the purse to extract some gold, when Humbert snatched the bag off her.

'Mine now,' he said.

Tara opened her mouth to utter a protest, but Mawgan laid his hand firmly on her arm. 'Yes, yours now.'

Tara snapped her mouth shut, disappointed there was nothing she could do. Zihna had said not to undervalue the power it held, but now they would never know what that was. She had also said not to underestimate the weakest of the gifts. Had they done just that? She sighed deeply. Tiredness overwhelmed her. Why couldn't anyone in this place just tell them what they needed to know straight out and not just hint at everything? Even Zalen hid things from them, she could tell. How did she know for sure they could trust anyone?

'I think I'll go and sit for awhile,' she said, 'before we continue the journey. It's tiring travelling the leys.'

'Of course,' agreed Mawgan looking concerned. 'Shall we play another game of *boules*?' Humbert looked pleased at this suggestion, and picked up the set of six larger and one smaller ball.

'I'm tired too,' said Jared, yawning. 'I'll go with Tara to rest.' He followed her into the main living room and everyone else went back outside.

Tara, weak with exhaustion, hoped Jared didn't want to talk. She decided to ignore him and feigned an examination of the room in an, *I'm busy don't bother me,* sort of way, when she heard the most beautiful music coming in through the open window.

'Braedon?' queried Jared.

'I think he plays beautifully,' said Tara and she scrambled up into a chair to enjoy its soothing tone.

'Tara...Jared! Taaraa!' shouted someone in the distance. It sounded like Mawgan.

'Tara!' boomed the voice of Humbert, and Tara was suddenly alert. She sat up shocked and immediately began to cough. An acrid smell of burning stung her nose cavities and she could feel the heat of a fire, which stretched in a line right across the room separating her and Jared from the door. The smoke quickly built up, drifting towards them.

Tara scrambled down from her chair. Jared was also awake and had jumped down. How on earth this could have happened and they not notice, she didn't know. The flames rapidly spread and Tara heard a whoosh as they spread to the curtains.

Jared had a fit of coughing. 'Is there another way out?' His voice caught in his throat and he could hardly be heard.

'No!' roared Humbert. 'I will come for you.'

Tara viewed the flames, which licked up the curtains, leaping across to the wooden beams and cutting them off from the window. The flames leapt too high even for Humbert. She shielded her face. 'No, it's too dangerous. We'll have to use Scathantar.' She took the mirror from the bag.

'But you don't know where it will take you,' shrieked Niamh.

'You have no choice,' shouted Mawgan over the roar of the flames, 'hopefully it does not take you too far. Try to make your way to where the five rivers meet. We will find you there. And watch out! The duergar bewitched you with his music.

Marvaanagh is behind this for sure.'

'Okay,' said Tara. The duergar, she thought with horror. This was all her fault. She had insisted on bringing him here, they had all warned her and it had been a trick after all.

'Le-Leanne is here,' spluttered Jared. 'She'll h-have to come with us.' He coughed again and moved closer to Tara.

Tara sighed, not more nonsense, they could do without it right now.

'Come here, close to us,' said Jared to Leanne.

Tara tried to ignore him, and huddling away from the searing heat, they put their heads together, looking into Scathantar as she held it horizontally. The faces that looked back at them had expressions of trepidation. Tara didn't know what to expect, for all she knew they might well end up in Dumnonia. She wished as hard as she could they didn't land too far.

A flash of light ensued followed by a huge jolt. For a moment, Tara thought she glimpsed the face of an angelic child behind them in the mirror.

The heat of the fire still burned her face as Tara briefly took in her new surroundings; they had landed in a small glade among some trees. The transfer had been instant and Tara let out a long sigh of relief at not having to go through the same thing as when travelling the ley. She put the mirror back into its bag. The breeze cooled her scorched skin and she held up her face to it.

'Phew!' said Jared. 'I'm not sorry to be out of that fire.' He looked to the side of him. Are you all right, Leanne?'

'More importantly, where are we?' Tara asked, not waiting for him to receive his imaginary answer. 'In the middle of nowhere by the looks of it.'

Well then, let's explore a bit and try to find out where we are.'

They clambered over fallen tree trunks and tangled under-growth, until through the remaining few trees, they could see a slope. They were high up, most likely on top of another hill fort or earthworks. After that, it was anybody's guess.

'I think maybe we should walk on a bit,' said Jared. 'We might not be far from Five Rivers.'

They climbed over the remaining undergrowth and set off down the slope. Tara hoped there would be a path when they reached the bottom. She began to contemplate where they could be. A thought came into her head and she couldn't shake it. Maybe her intuition was at work again. No, it sounded stupid, she was clutching at straws, but then… In the end, she decided to put it to Jared.

'Do you think it's possible Scathantar transported us somewhere else along the ley?' she asked at last, as they neared the bottom of the hill.

'Dunno really,' said Jared shrugging his shoulders.

'Well, we've been travelling along the line of the ley since we set out. The mound is on a ley and is near Vrogoly Forest. Rath Sarog and the Five Rivers Gateway are too, Princess Gwyn said. Maybe we're still on the ley somewhere, not in it obviously, but over it.' She raised her eyebrows questioningly. 'It's just a thought. Call it my intuition. If you look back, you'll see we landed on a hill fort so it could be there's even another gateway here somewhere. Even if there was, we wouldn't know when it opened or if it would take us in the right direction.'

'Well, we have to take your intuition seriously according to Princess Gwyn,' teased Jared. He looked at her and grinned. He must have seen Tara wasn't in a grinning mood, so he continued. 'Okay, say you're right. We were walking southwards. So…are we now north or are we south of the five rivers?'

Tara grimaced. 'I haven't a clue, but at least we're down to two choices. Actually, we might be down to one. When we were travelling south, we walked downhill remember. Now it's more rolling. I think we should go northwards.'

'Hmm, that's true I suppose,' said Jared. 'The sun should be behind us going to the west. Let's try to find a path – we'll decide where to go from there.'

Tara admired him for his logic. 'We'd better get a move on though, look!'

Jared followed her pointed finger to where mist lay on top of the hills; pockets of it now swirled among the trees ahead. Without hesitation, Tara tramped on through heaps of fallen leaves. Maybe on the other side of these trees lay a path. She stumbled as the mist became thicker. Soon they would be walking blindly. She dearly hoped this was not Marvaanagh at work again, but it was hard to tell.

'Take Swifan out, Jared. Just in case,' she said.

'Okay, will do.'

Jared had just removed it from its scabbard when he suddenly grabbed Tara's arm pulling her back. Tara heard what he'd heard, the baying of hounds and saw rustling in the trees ahead. They exchanged terrified glances. Tara's heart thumped hard in her chest.

'The Wild Hunt?' gasped Jared. But it sounded like a question.

'What do you mean,' asked Tara. The baying became louder and with it a thundering of hooves.

'It's the Wild Hunt. Leanne says it is.'

'Quick,' said Jared. 'This way…follow Leanne.'

How stupid, Tara thought, but at a loss to know what else to do, she ran behind. They ran headlong into some bushes. The hunt, if was indeed that and she decided it must be, was almost upon them.

'On the ground,' cried Jared. He threw himself down and Tara followed suit. 'Leanne says, keep still, hide your eyes and don't look up.'

Tara put her hands over her face. Underneath her, she could feel the vibrations of horse and hounds. Quaking, she heard the sound of a hunting horn amid the barking dogs and the dreadful pounding of hooves. Dust and leaves blew over them. Surely, they would be trampled to death, they were so close.

And then it was over. The din lessened. Tara looked through her fingers just in time to see a straggling hound fly past her – enormous, white, the size of a calf, with glistening red ears. Through the trees in a gap in the mist, there was a flash of antlers. The baying ebbed away into the distance.

They waited for a minute or two before pulling themselves to their feet. Jared faced the other way as if listening to Leanne. He turned with a petrified look. 'Someone will die tomorrow,' he said. 'Leanne says if you see the Wild Hunt, that's what happens.'

'Well, we didn't actually see it,' said Tara, wishing Jared wouldn't listen to someone who wasn't even there. 'All we saw was one hound.' This was getting too silly. Jared probably made up the whole thing about someone dying as part of his bewitchment. Still it had been frightening.

They tramped back to the path. The mist rapidly lifted and they managed to find a road, which looked like a major route. The dust indicated the Wild Hunt travelled in the opposite direction. Tara wiped her brow, realising it dripped with the sweat of fear.

After walking a short while, they could see turrets in the far distance.

'Do you think that's Caer Searesby?' asked Tara.

'Leanne says you're right and it is Caer Searesby,' Jared said nodding.

'But what do *you* think?' asked Tara. Jared was becoming far too reliant on his imagination for her liking

'Well, as Leanne knows this realm, I think we should believe her.'

Tara groaned and led the way onto the pathway. Cautiously, they kept to the side of the path just in case they quickly needed to hide. Hungry, Tara realised they had no food with them. It shouldn't be long until they met up with the others though. She remembered someone saying Rath Sarog was situated about an hour from where the five rivers met. The others would be walking downhill, so they should be more than halfway there by now, if they had left right away that is.

A few minutes later, and thinking they would never get there, Tara saw a flash of white out of the corner of her eye. Two seconds later, the stag leapt out on the pathway in front of them. He bobbed his head at her, trotting up and down on the same spot.

Tara was trying make out what he was attempting to show her when Jared whipped past her and stroked his neck.

'Leanne says he's trying to be friendly, I think he wants us to ride on him.'

'You can't ride a deer, Jared,' said Tara horrified. But the stag kept jiggling his antlers.

'We both can't ride on him, for sure,' said Jared. 'You go and Leanne and I will catch up. Someone needs to tell the others we're all right and to wait for us. Maybe he'll come back and fetch us.'

'Perhaps Leanne should come with me.' It popped out before Tara had time to think about it. She didn't know why she said it, except she forgot Leanne wasn't real and was thinking purely of her safety.

'Leanne says to say thank you, but she can't leave me. So you'd better go. We'll be fine, I have Swifan remember.'

Nodding her head in agreement, Tara wondered how she would climb up. She looked around for something to stand on. Showing no fear, Jared took the antlers of the stag and led him to a large rock. With a bit of a struggle, her long dress getting in the way, Tara hitched up the skirts, stepped onto the rock and struggled onto the stag's broad back. She wrapped her arms tightly around his neck.

He set off immediately, soon gathering speed. Not daring to turn around to wave, Tara hung on. What she wasn't prepared for was how fast the stag would move as his feet were indeed swift. She clung to him as he careered along, knowing he was unlikely to slow or stop until they reached Five Rivers.

Like a merry-go-round horse, they travelled over the undulating path, occasionally soaring over a bigger hill causing a sinking feeling in Tara's stomach.

After a few minutes, she saw with relief the three inter-twining rivers. Surely, it couldn't be far now, she thought, but they galloped on and on. The stag flew along, his feet hardly brushing the ground, out of the corner of her eye, the fields and woodland flashed by them and the rivers disappeared from view.

Tara hoped Jared was all right, she had a sudden rush of guilt for leaving them…him behind. Scathantar had transported them a long way. It was probably wise she had thought to concentrate on not going too far when looking at their reflections. If Scathantar worked out that not too far was the next earthworks, if she hadn't put any thought into it they might indeed have ended up in Dumnonia.

After what seemed an age the rivers came back into view. The stag pulled to a stop at the edge of a pathway. In the distance, Tara could see a horse coming her way. On it, sat Niamh. Mawgan strode on one side of it holding the reins with Zalen on the other side. Something wasn't right about the scene.

As they came nearer, Tara saw they all wore solemn expres-sions. Lucy's swollen face indicated she had been crying, and she hung onto the horse's bridle. A shiver rippled along Tara's spine penetrating her very bones. The fire, of course…had they been injured?

She slid down off the stag's back and watched as he turned and trotted off back down the path. Hopefully, she thought, to collect Jared.

Tara ran up the pathway and peered at Niamh, Lucy, Mawgan and Zalen in turn. They all looked fine and had no injuries she could see, so why the concerned faces? Why didn't anyone speak? Mawgan glanced up at Niamh and back at Tara. Tara looked up at Niamh who stared down at her, but not at her, in fact over her shoulder. Tara's heart sank into her boots. Niamh was blind.

Chapter Nineteen

Tara stared, horrified.

'It's okay,' said Niamh. 'I just can't see. It was scary at first, but I'm getting used to it now.'

'The fire…?' Tara immediately knew it was her fault, she had insisted they take Braedon to Rath Sarog.

'No, no, it wasn't the fire,' said Niamh vehemently.

'Bewitchment,' stated Mawgan, 'the scarf we think.'

Tara fell to her knees and put her head in hands. It *was* her fault. She, who was supposed to be taking care of them, had caused Niamh's blindness by being careless. Humbert's home had burned down too, because she had insisted on helping Braedon, and all because she had been angry – was angry. Anger ate at her, several reasons why popped up into her head, she was angry at being left out, angry at Jared for making new friends, angry at not being taken seriously all the time, and mostly, angry because she didn't have a dad and her mum suffered because of it. Now Niamh…blind…

'I'm so, so sorry,' she cried, her eyes filled with burning tears, which spilled through her fingers. 'It's all my fault.'

Mawgan came to her side, and taking her hands from her face, he wiped her eyes with his hanky. 'No, it is not, my dear. Queen Marvaanagh has done this terrible thing. She would have found some way.'

'I thought because I had the bracelet I was safe,' said Niamh. 'But it must mean it doesn't protect from injury, only from death. Zalen thinks that anyway. And that's what Princess Gwyn said, actually.'

'I'm looking after her,' declared Lucy. She glanced around. 'Where's Jared?'

'We couldn't all…I mean…that is…me, Jared and – and Leanne, couldn't all fit on the stag at the same time. So now the stag has gone back for them...er, him.'

Mawgan helped Tara to her feet and lifted Niamh down off the horse. Lucy caught her arm and led her over to Tara who tightly hugged her.

'I think we should take this opportunity to rest a while and eat something,' said Mawgan, 'while we wait for Jared.'

'I *was* hungry, but I doubt I can eat anything now.' Tara sniffed, feeling wretched.

'Come on,' coaxed Niamh gently. 'You should eat something.'

Tara hung her head, how could Niamh be so nice to her. She lifted her chin and smiled her agreement, before remembering Niamh couldn't see her. Stroking her arm she said, 'Yes, let's eat.'

By the time they found somewhere to sit under some sycamore trees and had settled down and unpacked the food, Jared arrived on the stag's back. He slid off. The stag wandered off, but still stayed within sight.

'That was cool,' said Jared laughing. 'Never ridden a stag before, or anything else for that matter.'

Tara told Jared about Niamh.

'How do we fix her?' he asked.

'The only way would be to find the scarf and give it back to Niamh,' said Zalen.

'Then we'll have to do that. What's the plan now?' asked Jared.

'We need to enter the castle and challenge Marvaanagh. We must demand to see Donella. After all, she is my betrothed. We must insist on the truth,' said Mawgan.

Niamh twiddled with her hair. 'I have a feeling it won't be as easy as that. Marvaanagh is trying to stop us from even getting there.'

'Yes,' agreed Tara. 'She's trying to kill us all. She won't just let us walk in.'

'Well, in that case we shall find another way in,' said Mawgan quite firmly. 'We just need a good plan...'

They packed up their belongings. Mawgan decided to leave

the horse behind and travel on by foot as it wasn't far. He left it in the trees. As they walked away, Tara glanced back to see the stag had stayed with it.

They had only tramped a short distance when Tara's feet began to sink into the soggy ground, the leaves underfoot mushy and smelling of damp – the whole area one big bog.

'This is most strange,' muttered Mawgan and he walked ahead a short way and looked around. 'Another enchantment?'

'I recognise this place,' said Zalen with fearful tones in his voice. 'This is the Gogges. But the Gogges lie in the north, there is an underground spring there...and a well...that houses...that houses...a...a worm. Yet here they lie. Queen Marvaanagh must have the ability of practicing great magic.'

'It might be a glamour spell,' said Tara knowledgeably. 'Like with the mushrooms.'

'Yet it feels real enough,' said Zalen. 'Queen Marvaanagh is capable of this, though it would take forward planning. She can control the weather, as we have seen. If the Gogges are here, so is the worm.'

'Worm! What harm can a worm do?' asked Lucy, giggling.

Mawgan put his hand on her shoulder. 'This is not the type of worm you are used to seeing. Alas, we must move on and attempt to pass it.'

'How dangerous is this worm?' Tara knew it didn't bode well; yet another trial to overcome.

'Very, so we must go carefully,' said Mawgan. 'And if the worm appears, you must avoid its saliva, it is deadly poison.'

'Can't we go around it,' asked Tara.

'I am afraid not,' said Mawgan, scratching his neck nervously as he weighed up the situation. 'A river lies at either side. We have no choice, we have to walk on.'

As they continued onwards, they moved closer together for protection. The trees had become denser. Like in Vrogoly Forest, it had the same eerie quietness, which comes just before something horrible happens.

Because the path narrowed, the pace slowed for a few metres until a glade open up in front of them. A huge pool of dark swirling water set in the ground, blocked their way. Large slabs of stone of several levels edged it, making steps.

Mawgan put his finger to his lips and motioned to them to be silent. Together they crept slowly forward. Mawgan took the lead and Tara put her hands on Niamh's shoulders to help guide her, while Lucy held her hand.

Jared drew Swifan from its scabbard. Zalen pulled at Mawgan's cloak to attract his attention and silently pointed to a gap in the dense undergrowth to the left. They must go that way once they got past the well, thought Tara. Jared bent down as if to whisper instructions to the invisible Leanne.

'Ouch!' Lucy, who had stumbled on a sharp stone, suddenly cried out in pain, and bent down to rub her ankle. She looked around at them an apology plain in her eyes. They all froze, everyone holding their breath.

For a few seconds – nothing, then a gurgling noise as the water in the well began to churn. Tara trembled as an enormous green, snake-like dragon, burst from it. Pointed spines stretched along its back, its iridescent scales glistening in a beam of sunlight. It rose above them, uncoiling its massive head. Its huge mouth opened revealing a set of vicious teeth and a long, thin, forked tongue, unrolled like a vine. The worm's questing snout twisted and turned, its tongue tasting the air as it honed in on their scent.

It slid out of the pool.

Tara cowered as it let out a tremendous roar, stretching its head towards the sky in anger, its long tail lashing around, hitting trees behind it – knocking them out of the ground. It swung its head back down fixing them with its beady eyes.

'Run!' cried Mawgan. 'Head for the gap!'

Mawgan drew his sword and darted to the right of the beast,

jumping up and down, waving his arms about, to try to draw its attention away from the others. He screamed and shouted until at last the worm twisted towards him, its head whipping around. A glob of saliva flew from its mouth barely missing Mawgan and landing on a tree. The foaming saliva began to sizzle and smoke. Jared turned to Tara and beckoned them on.

Tara pushed Niamh forward towards the gap in the under-growth, beyond which, the path wound. To her horror, Lucy didn't follow; instead, she dropped Niamh's hand and dashed to help Mawgan.

'Nooo!' screamed Tara. Niamh couldn't see what was happening and tried to turn back. Tara pushed her around.

'No, Niamh!' shouted Jared. 'Go on, keep moving, Tara!' And he bounded after Lucy waving Swifan in the air.

Niamh hesitated and Tara pushed her forward. She glanced behind her to see the worm now turning its attention to Lucy, who was slipping and sliding in the boggy ground, trying to find a firm footing. Zalen, who was standing on the edge of the scene, rushed towards her.

'Lucyyyy!' yelled Jared, as the worm swept down on her.

Tara watched helplessly, rigid with terror. An anxious look from Jared alerted her and she kept pushing Niamh towards the gap until she was safely out of the way.

Tara turned again to see Jared race towards Lucy waving Swifan around in the air to try to distract the worm.

Lucy attempted to run backwards, but the soft ground hampered her and she tripped over a tree root, falling flat on her back.

Zalen darted to Lucy's side.

Tara remembered Scathantar. She shouted and waved it around, hoping one of them would turn so she could throw it to them, but everyone remained glued to the worm's every move.

With a screech, a huge raven appeared sweeping over the head of the worm. Zalen began to pull Lucy out of the way while the others stood guard. The worm had turned from her, whipping its head upwards towards the raven, as it did, a great glob of white foaming saliva flew from its mouth and landed on Lucy, most of it on her cloak, but a small amount hit her face.

The raven again swooped down on the worm. Zalen took one look at it and his arms came up to protect his head. It soon became clear the raven was trying to attack the worm, not them. Zalen seemed to come to his senses and grew to his full size. He swept Lucy up and carried her back to Tara and Niamh. He pulled a handkerchief from his pocket and swiftly wiped the saliva from Lucy's face and clothes, but it had already begun to sizzle, burning a hole in her cloak. Tara could see Lucy's face, scarlet, where the saliva had caught her cheek. 'Lucyyy!'

'I'm sorry,' Lucy managed to say before she fell unconscious.

Tara began to shake, tears scalding her eyes. She put her arm around Lucy's neck.

'Wake up, Lucy!'

'The poison!' said Zalen as he shrank back to his normal size. 'We must get some healing water from the well or she will die.'

The worm gave a thunderous roar, uprooted a tree with its tail, and began using it as a club, banging it down hard on the ground. 'Cut off the end of its tail,' yelled Zalen to Jared.

Mawgan thrust his sword at the worm's neck, the raven still attacking from above. Jared moved around to the back of the worm, having to duck the thrashing tree, which it now slung, about narrowly missing him.

'Tara, you have to be brave,' said Zalen firmly. 'We need to get Niamh and Lucy further up the path to safety. I cannot grow again, it is too soon.'

A sob caught in Tara's throat, she choked it back and nodded, wiping at her tears. Finding strength she didn't know she had, Tara lifted Lucy from the ground. She carried her up the narrow path trying not to trip over the tangled undergrowth. Zalen took Niamh's arm and followed.

Once safely hidden in the trees, she put Lucy down.

'We need the well water and some of the worm's blood,' said Zalen.

Tara nodded. Opening her backpack, she took out two flasks and emptied their contents onto the ground. She ran back just in time to see Jared hacking at the worm's tail, and Mawgan darting about endeavouring to keep away from the poisonous saliva.

Swifan did its job well, slicing through the impossibly thick skin without too much trouble. At last, blood spurted from the tail, as the end of it came away. The worm lifted its head and howled, thrashing the rest of his tail from side to side in fury, splashing blood everywhere.

Tara saw her chance, and darted to the edge of the well, keeping one eye on the worm. An expression of horror crossed Mawgan's features and he waved her away. She shook her head and threw the other flask to him. 'Here, for the blood,' she cried. 'You must get some.'

Mawgan deftly caught it.

She bent down, filled the flask with well water, and ran back to Lucy.

Zalen shook his head gravely. 'Help me lift her head.'

Tara lifted Lucy's head, and Zalen put the bottle to her mouth. Most of the water dribbled out. Finally, she swallowed some. Zalen poured more water over her face.

'This will help her,' he said solemnly, 'for now.'

Tara ran back to the others. She had to see if she could help in some way. When she arrived at the pool, she saw Mawgan throw the flask to Jared. 'Get some of the blood!' he cried.

Catching the flask, Jared collected some blood, while Mawgan kept his eye on the worm, which was still reeling from its injury. Once Jared had the blood, they both turned and sprinted towards Tara.

The worm stopped howling. Tara saw it swing around and grabbing the tail stump from the ground, it began to occupy itself in attaching it back on, periodically dipping it in and out of the healing well water. The raven flew off.

Tara led them to where Lucy lay. Jared fell to his knees next to her. 'Is she going to be all right?' he cried, his voice quavering.

'I hope so,' said Zalen. But he didn't sound convinced.

Jared handed Zalen the flask of blood. Zalen opened it and tipped some blood over her face.

'Yuk,' said Tara.

'This will save her life,' said Zalen. 'If we're not too late.'

'Will the worm come after us?'

'No, Tara. It will stay at the pool.'

Everyone grew silent as an anxious five minutes passed by. Then just as Niamh began to cry, Lucy at last opened her eyes to see everyone leaning over her.

'W-what happened?'

'The worm's saliva hit you, Luce,' said Jared with surprising tenderness.

Lucy struggled to sit up and seeing the hole in her cloak whimpered, 'Oh no, Mum's going to kill me going home in such a mess.'

'She nearly didn't have to,' said Jared ironically.

Tara laughed nervously, but knew no one thought it remotely funny. Lucy almost died. The worst experience so far in the Otherworld, Tara hoped she would never ever have to see another worm as long as she lived, not even an earthworm.

'For heaven's sake, what do you think you were doing, rushing up like that?' continued Jared. 'You were supposed to go with Niamh.'

'I-I'm really sorry, but the worm was going to hurt Prince Mawgan and it was all my fault.'

'Oh and you, just a little girl, was going to stop it all on your own…right. Even Leanne had the sense to follow Tara and Niamh, and she's only seven!'

'Never mind about that right now,' said Mawgan kindly. 'I am sure she has learnt her lesson. How do you feel, Lucy?'

'A bit woozy and sick.'

Zalen gave her some more of the well water. 'Let us see if you can stand.'

Tara and Mawgan helped her up. She wobbled and fell towards Mawgan.

'We should take this opportunity to leave,' said Mawgan. 'Come, I will carry you on my back.'

Jared helped Lucy climb onto Mawgan's back. The rest of them gathered up their things.

'Can't we use the blood to help Niamh see again,' asked Lucy.

'No,' answered Zalen. 'The blood will only heal normal injury. Niamh's injury is caused by magic and that can only be undone by finding the scarf.'

They trekked on out of the Gogges, towards the castle. A river lay on either side of them, neither looked threatening, but peacefully meandered on towards the other three rivers. Even though it was still daylight, Tara knew it grew late. It must be early evening. She could swear the days went quicker here than they did at home.

Less than half a mile, she thought, would get them to the castle, but she didn't want to go on. How could they face Marvaanagh with Lucy sick and Niamh blind? Too much had happened. She couldn't face another confrontation with anything or anyone right now. Most of all they needed time to think. Queen Marvaanagh was much more powerful than any of them had imagined. They had to have a very good plan before going to the castle.

Mawgan must have read her mind. 'On reflection,' he said. 'I do not think we should go to Caer Searesby until the morning. Lucy is weak and will need a few hours to recover fully. We cannot leave her behind and we all need to rest after our ordeal.'

They all agreed and Tara didn't feel she could do anymore fighting today. If things had been bad up to now, they could only get worse. 'Where will we sleep,' she asked.

'There is an old cottage not far from here,' said Zalen. 'Travellers sometimes stop there to rest. And it is well away from the village, where the queen is sure to have spies.'

'Then lead the way and let us go forth to it,' agreed Mawgan. 'By doing so, Queen Marvaanagh may well believe we have been prevented from going further by the Gogges Worm. At dawn, we shall take her by surprise.'

The cottage wasn't far, well hidden in some trees. Mawgan took Lucy inside and Tara led Niamh in behind them. After settling Lucy on a bed of clean straw, Zalen suggested Mawgan and Jared should gather some firewood. They had nothing else to keep them warm and the night would be cold. Luckily, there looked to be plenty around.

Inside the one-roomed cottage, at least it was dry. A couple of rickety chairs and a three-legged stool made up the whole of the furniture, though plenty more straw lay piled in the corners. Once there must have been fires burning in the grate as they found some kindling lying on the hearth and a few logs.

Zalen took two flint stones from his pocket and struck them over a bit of straw until sparks fell. The straw began to smoulder. He placed a few pieces of kindling on top, and a couple of small logs, the fire soon roared up the chimney.

Niamh opened her backpack and groping around inside took out some bread and cheese. Tara and Zalen helped her unpack the rest of the food.

Jared and Mawgan returned soon after with large bundles of firewood and they all settled down to eat.

'I'm feeling much better now,' said Lucy, after they'd finished.

'Me too,' said Jared. 'That worm was enormous. Fighting it was the most incredible thing ever, though I can't say I enjoyed the experience that much. I didn't think about it while it was happening, but now well...in truth, it was scary.' He shuddered, staring into the fire.

Tara didn't speak. It was an horrendous experience and she tried not to go over what happened in the Gogges, but couldn't help it. She wasn't surprised when Mawgan proposed playing some word games to lighten the mood. Lucy suggested I Spy and explained to Mawgan how to play it.

Later they all told funny stories. Mawgan told one about how when he was seven years old he had wanted to look inside a bird nest. He'd climbed a huge tree, but couldn't get down again. He'd screamed for help until one of his uncle's guards had heard him, and half of the army turned up at the bottom of the tree to help rescue him.

Jared told them all about the day Lucy went missing on Salisbury Plain, and the police had been called. Her parents found her asleep under a tree, only a few yards from the house. Still, it meant that now he had to go everywhere with her, which was why he was here now, and he wasn't sorry about that, for all their troubles.

One by one, they fell asleep. The last thing Tara remembered seeing was Mawgan and Zalen talking quietly together, most likely making plans. When she awoke, the sun streamed in through the window, dust particles floating in the rays. Rubbing her eyes, she sat up and looked around. Zalen had gone.

Chapter Twenty

While they ate the rest of the food, they talked about Zalen having sneaked away; they all suspected he had gone on to Caer Searesby.

'Traitor!' cried Jared. 'And he took the healing water, it was in his backpack!'

'He might not have gone there at all,' said Tara. 'He might have just gone back to the palace.'

'Coward,' growled Jared. 'Anyway I doubt he would want to pass the worm again. No, he's a traitor.'

'We shouldn't judge, he might not be anything of the sort, and probably forgot he had the healing water,' Tara said, angry at Jared's presumption. Just when she was thinking Jared was all right, he just became the same old Jared.'

Lucy's cheeks glowed pink again. She had recovered well, thank goodness. That was one person less to have to worry about, thought Tara. Jared on the loss of the healing water had checked for the flask with the worm's blood. It was still there – congealed, but not totally useless. Mawgan told them dried worm's blood could still be effective.

They formed a plan. It wasn't much of one. But at least they had one. Mawgan had told them of a secret passageway that led from the buttery near the kitchen, up to a gallery near Donella's quarters. They would make for the postern gate at the back of the castle. Lucy would lead Niamh.

They were as ready as they would ever be, so set off. Tara felt much refreshed. The tiredness had lifted, and soon she would find out what happened to her sister and father. She wondered what her sister was called now. Although Niamh had another name, she would always be Niamh to Tara. Tara's missing sister surely would be used to her new name too. It was all so complicated.

The back of the castle lay before them, huge and magnificent. Its grey outer walls, which Mawgan called the outer ward, had four formidable towers with arrow holes and a number of smaller towers in between. One of the five rivers had been diverted to make a moat. Mawgan said that around the other side of the castle, a barbican prevented access to the drawbridge. Even if they managed to get past this, there was a portcullis, which would surely be down, preventing them from entering.

They now stood in front of the postern gate, set in the wall above the water. Tara stood staring at it. How would they get to it across the moat?

'I hope it is still there,' said Mawgan.

'What's still there,' asked Tara.

'The boat Donella and I sometimes played on as children,' he said, looking right then left along the moat. 'I think we may have left it down that way.'

They walked along the river and on the opposite side spied a large rowing boat among some reeds.

'I will swim over and fetch it,' said Mawgan.

Tara looked at the boat. It was quite far out, but she could swim all the way without coming up for air. She contemplated how she would bring the boat back. Rowing it back wasn't an option as she would easily be seen, but she could tow it back if she could find the same strength she had when she and Lucy were in the river.

'No, I'll go,' she offered. 'I can swim underwater.'

'Not all that way, Tara, it is too far,' said Mawgan. 'No one can swim underwater that long, except the water folk.'

'I can do it.'

Jared looked shocked. 'No way, Tara.'

'You have to believe me, both of you, it's one of those gifts Princess Gwyn said I had. I can do it…easily. How do you think we survived the river? You have to let me do it. I can stand the cold too.'

'Then, we will trust you,' said Mawgan.

'She can't do it!' Jared protested. 'She's just a girl.'

'I think she can do it, girl or not,' declared Lucy.

Tara was already removing her cloak, jacket and boots. Finding nothing suitable to wear for swimming in the backpack given to her, she left her dress on. It would be no trouble as it was as light as silk. She did find another dress similar to the one she wore, so could change later.

Before anyone had a chance to protest further, Tara dropped down into the river. She smiled at everyone before ducking under the surface.

The water was calm, and after the initial shock of the cold, she was soon swimming confidently and so deep, she could even see the large pebbles on the river floor beneath her. She hoped no one standing on the ramparts of the castle could also see her. Though she doubted they would expect someone to be able to swim underwater for as long as she could.

Halfway across, Tara saw her fingers were webbing again. What was more, a tingly feeling rippled through her legs down to her toes and her swimming became even more fluid. A few trout swam past her and she felt comfortable swimming along with them.

She loved being in the moat, and when she at last reached the boat, was reluctant to raise her head above the water, she was enjoying it so much. But the others would need to know she had arrived safely.

Tara popped up her head, and seeing everyone standing on the bank near some bushes, waved to them. They all stared open mouthed at her as she came up, and Tara couldn't help feeling proud to be able to do her bit to help. It might go some way to making up for her previous blunders.

Giving another quick wave, Tara grabbed the rope and dived down underwater again. Instinctively, she put the hoop of the rope around her neck and swam back. Even though slowed by the weight of the boat, her return was just as fluid. She at last surfaced at the other side, laughing. Her laugh faded away as she saw the stunned faces of Lucy and Jared. Even Niamh, who nothing could faze these days, frowned. Mawgan stared at her, a flabbergasted look on his face.

'What's the matter? What's happened?' Tara asked, glancing back at the castle, concerned someone may have spotted her.

No one spoke. It was as if they had lost the power of speech. At last Lucy gasped, 'Tara, you've turned into a mermaid!'

Tara swung around, to her dismay, she found her legs had gone, and in their place, she had an aqua-blue, iridescent fishtail, which swished around in the water. She hadn't noticed, as it felt so normal.

'I've been bewitched!' she cried. She held up her hands, staring at the delicate webbing between her fingers. It was natural. She didn't know how she knew this, but she did. 'No, I'm not bewitched…this is me…'

'It's all right,' said Mawgan. 'We'll help you out and all will be well.'

Tara noticed her wet dress clung to her, and was thankful her long hair covered most of her body. She lifted up her arms and Mawgan and Jared pulled her from the water and laid her on the bank.

'Here,' said Mawgan passing over her clothes, and backpack. He turned to the others and said, 'Let us leave Tara, she requires privacy. Trust me on this. Your friend will be fine.'

Tara watched as they moved away from her, leaving only Niamh behind. She covered her fishtail with her cloak. Last time her fingers had webbed they had returned to normal once out of the water. She was hopeful the same thing would happen now. Tara thought back to the merrows, Uncle Fergus was with them, or someone who resembled him. Further back, she recalled how Uncle Fergus had taught her how to swim, and encouraged her in the sport. Uncle Fergus surely had something to do with these realms. And somehow…so did Tara. She was also a child of the fae, she was certain of it.

'Are you all right, Tara,' asked Niamh.

'Yes, I'm fine,' Tara replied. 'I'm a merrow…I think…well at least part merrow. I don't know how or why, but I think that's what I am.'

After a short while, the strange tingling sensation ran back up her tail. Tara wiggled it and watched as it dissolved before her eyes revealing her legs.

'I'm me again, Niamh,' she said.

'Oh I wish I could see you as a mermaid, Tara.'

'I have a feeling you will once you get your sight back, it won't be long Niamh. It won't be long now.'

She grabbed her backpack and rooted in it for the dress she had seen earlier, and put it on and her cloak too, to help her warm up.

She called the others back over. Lucy came to her side staring at her in awe. 'You're a mermaid, Tara. I wish I was a mermaid.'

Jared just stared at her, as if seeing her in a new light.

Mawgan had turned his attention to the boat. 'I see that it is still used,' he said. 'Good, we must make haste – not tarry too long.' He climbed into the boat and putting out his hand, first helped Niamh, Lucy and then Tara.

'Get in then, Leanne,' said Jared.

Mawgan was at a loss what to do. But Jared, ignoring him, carried on helping Leanne. He almost convinced Tara she *was* real. Anyone would think Jared was actually helping someone into the boat, in the way of a good mime act.

At last Jared stepped down into the boat himself. Mawgan and Tara took an oar each, so Jared could be on guard. They rowed along the diverted river and into the moat.

As they neared the middle of the moat, a commotion above put them on guard. Grislic goblins appeared along the battlements and within a few seconds, rocks landed in the water around them, making great splashes.

Tara looked up in time to see a rock headed towards the back of the boat where Jared sat. Jared held up Swifan, attempting to shield his head with the dagger. The rock flew away from him landing harmlessly in the water. With a look of great surprise and then a grin, Jared jumped into the middle of the boat and swinging his arm around in a wide circular motion, deflected more rocks. Meanwhile, Mawgan and Tara taking heart, rowed like mad.

They at last reached the other side, but not before a rock had holed the boat, it slowly began to take in water.

Mawgan jumped out onto a step, and tried to push open the door. It wouldn't budge.

Tara looked at the keyhole, and suddenly it changed shape. 'Try Swifan.' Everyone looked at her as if she were mad. 'Try Swifan, I think it's a master key...'

Mawgan looked again at the lock and held his hand out for Swifan, which Jared passed over a little hesitantly. Mawgan pushed the blade into the lock and it turned it. The door opened. He gave Swifan back to Jared. 'There are stone steps just beneath the water,' he said. 'Come, I will assist you.' Mawgan held his hand out towards Lucy, and she stepped onto the steps and through the door. Tara helped Niamh out and Mawgan pulled her through. Tara went next and Jared urged Leanne to follow. Jared meanwhile was still swinging his arm around.

'Now,' shouted Mawgan, and Jared jumped out of the boat. But already the rock throwing had stopped.

They stepped into the outer ward. The inner part of the castle lay in front of them. Like the outside, it had similar grey walls, arrow slits, and even four large towers. Tara wondered if Donella was confined in one of them and if she could see them. Strangely, there wasn't a sign of any goblins, as if they had all gone to ground.

It was deathly quiet. Tara's intuition didn't let her down,

something was about to happen and suddenly they heard galloping hooves – not a normal sound of a horse's hooves, but a sickeningly thunderous, terrifying noise.

'Leanne says get back out, it's a Dullahan!' said Jared anxiously.

Mawgan stiffened and looked at them with horror in his eyes. 'It is possible. Make haste now, back through the gate.'

Nearest, Tara stepped back through the gate to see the boat slowly sinking in the middle of the moat. 'Down the steps,' Mawgan shouted with urgency.

Tara hurried down several steps into the water leaving room for everyone else. Mawgan came next, Lucy came behind and she and Jared helped Niamh. Jared came through last. He stood on the top step.

'Shut the door, Jared,' shouted Mawgan.

'I can't! Leanne—' objected Jared.

'We have no time, Jared.'

'Don't be stupid and shut the door, Jared. Leanne isn't real!' insisted Tara.

'No! No!' cried Jared and the door suddenly slammed shut.

'Oh no!' he cried again. 'Leanne is trapped inside. She did it herself...' He covered his face with his hands. Lucy put her hand out to him.

It was as if a million ants crawled up Tara's spine and down her limbs, her heart skipped a beat and then another, and the sudden realisation she had done something terrible descended upon her like a dark storm. As the hooves thundered past, it reminded her of the Wild Hunt. Someone would die. Even if Leanne wasn't real, Jared could see her...she was real to him. Emotion welled up inside Tara until she thought she would choke, and tears ran down her face. She sobbed. It was all too much.

A couple of minutes went past while she and Jared composed themselves.

Jared wiped his eyes with his sleeves. 'W-what happens if you see the Dullahan.'

'The Dullahan is a headless horseman who rides a black steed. If he stops in front of you, I am afraid you will die. We do not see him in these parts, only in the far realms of Iwernia, across the sea. This is Marvaanagh's doing, somehow she has managed to conjure him up—'

'I don't think it stopped,' Niamh, quickly interjected. 'I heard it carry on galloping...really.'

'No, it didn't stop, did it?' said Jared. 'It might not have been able to see her.'

'No,' agreed Mawgan. But Tara could see the anguish that lay in his eyes.

'How do we get past?' asked Niamh. 'We can't stay here.'

'No, we have to go in,' insisted Jared. 'We need to see if Leanne is okay.'

Everyone went quiet as the sound of hooves once more became louder. Then they receded into the distance.

'The Dullahan must be riding around and around the outer ward, we have no chance of passing by it,' replied Mawgan. 'Unless...unless...would anyone by chance have any gold?'

'Gold?' said Tara.

'Yes, if you throw it down in front of the Dullahan, it will banish it.'

'Oh no, the Purse of Plenty! The Mordanta told us not to undervalue any of the gifts,' said Tara. 'Now look what we've gone and done.'

'It's my fault,' groaned Niamh. 'It was me who suggested giving the gold to Humbert.'

Tara had also agreed the gold be given to Humbert. It seemed everything that went wrong was her fault. 'What are we to do?'

'I have my bracelet,' said Niamh.

'No, Niamh, it protects you.'

Niamh ignored her and began pulling her bracelet off, then

changed her mind.

'I gave a solemn promise,' she said forlornly. She stood staring into the nothingness that was all she could see. 'Princess Gwyn said I mustn't take it off, or I could cause all our deaths, so I'm not going to.' And as the hooves once more became louder, she pushed past Jared, opened the door, and ran through it. Jared tried to grab her, but it was too late.

Without even thinking about it, they all followed her. Tara, last in, arrived just in time to see Niamh lying on the ground, her arm outstretched, her bracelet gleaming. The shiny black stallion hovered above her – its horrendous eyes, flaming red. The headless horseman sat upon it, dressed all in black, his glowing gruesome head resting on his lap.

Tara covered her mouth with her hand. She could have sworn it looked at her with its darting eyes. The grin stretching across its face was so hideous she thought she would faint. In his hand, he held what looked like a bony spine, which he used as a whip, trying to spur the horse onwards.

There was a shrill scream from Lucy. Something flew across the space and Lucy suddenly stopped in mid-scream. Tara turned to see her covered in blood. Lucy dropped to the ground. Tara glimpsed a bowl in the Dullahan's other hand as it hovered above Niamh, before fading away into nothing.

Mawgan dashed to Niamh and helped her up. Tara followed, and they led her back to the others. Jared meanwhile had raced to Lucy's side. Reaching them, Tara bent down to see if she was all right.

Lucy opened her eyes. 'Eww, he threw blood at me, am I going to die?'

'Erm…no,' said Mawgan, barely concealing a smile. 'You attracted his attention when you screamed.' He used his handkerchief to wipe some blood away.

'That's just so gross, Luce,' said Jared. 'What is it with you and blood?'

Tara stood up. Seeing Lucy was all right, she turned and threw her arms around Niamh. 'Niamh, that was a daft thing to do, you could have been killed.'

'I'm okay,' said Niamh. 'I just scraped my knees.' She bent down to rub them.

'Where's Leanne? asked Jared, looking perplexed. 'She's not here.'

Tara glanced around. 'Maybe she went into the castle.'

'Perhaps, this is so, Jared,' said Mawgan. 'We must make haste now, before more terror rains on us, and the grislic goblins appear again.'

Chapter Twenty-One

Mawgan led them across the outer ward to a small door. 'This leads to the buttery,' he whispered. They followed him along a dark narrow passage and at last came to a small room. 'Hurry,' he said. 'The sooner we go into the passage, the safer we will be.'

They could hear voices echoing behind them.

'Help me with this, Jared,' said Mawgan. Together, they pulled a great rack of wine forward. Luckily it didn't make too much noise. They all stepped into the secret passage just as the voices became louder. Mawgan shut the door behind them, leaving them in pitch darkness. 'Do not worry. I know this passageway well. Everyone, hold onto each other.'

He led the way and as Tara stumbled in the darkness, she had a taste of what it must be like for Niamh. They felt their way up the narrow winding stone staircase. At the top, Mawgan groped around and a door slowly opened, letting in some light. They stepped out into a long room, which Mawgan called the gallery, the sort of room Tara has seen when visiting castles. Portraits of people adorned the oak-lined walls, while a red patterned rug covered most of the floor.

'Donella's room is just along here.' Mawgan pointed to the end of the gallery.

They left the gallery and walked into a smaller hallway with a stone-flagged floor. Mawgan stopped outside a room and gently knocked on the door. No one answered, so he knocked again.

'Who – who is it,' said a trembling voice.

'It is me...Mawgan,'

'Oh, thank goodness, Mawgan. I am locked in!'

Mawgan tried to push the door open. Not having any luck, he turned to Jared who handed Swifan over without question. Mawgan placed Swifan into the lock and the door opened inwards revealing a large room with a girl standing in the middle, her hands to her face. Dressed in a tunic and trousers, similar to the ones Mawgan wore, her long hair was black and curly, reaching down to her waist. She looked astonishingly familiar, but then her hair was exactly like Niamh's.

As soon as Mawgan entered the room, Donella threw herself into his arms.

She let go of Mawgan and looked at each of them in turn. Her eyes rested on Niamh as she took in the similar hair. Then she peered at Tara curiously and smiled. 'You are the realm child, I believe,' she said to Tara.

'Gosh, no! It's Niamh actually.'

Donella looked at Niamh. 'Of – of course, I recognise that now.' Tara saw a blush spread over her face and neck. 'She is blind though?'

'Marvaanagh's magic,' said Niamh.

Tara looked at Donella. 'Princess Gwyn said you would have the answer to what happened to my sister and father...' She paused. 'When Niamh was a baby, someone exchanged her for my real sister and my father disappeared at the same time. It was ten years ago, when she was just one year old. We – we think Niamh is your sister...' At this point, it all sounded so weak to Tara, especially as Niamh looked nothing like Donella except for the hair, she couldn't go on.

Donella had recovered from her mistake, but seemed to agree. 'I am sorry to disappoint you, but I do not have a sister and never have. I would be six years old at the time and I would remember. But no time to talk now,' she said. 'We must leave here. My aunt will know you will come to me.'

'Back to the secret passage then,' agreed Mawgan. 'I feel it is the safest place.'

As they turned to leave the room, they spotted two grislic goblins heading their way from each end of the hallway – their old enemies, Dargen and Grud. They were trapped.

Jared drew Swifan holding it out in front of him, and Tara

took out Scathantar. She turned the mirror around and thrust it into Grud's face. At the same moment, she wished him far away. In an instant, he was gone. Tara darted over to Dargen and while he stood dumbfounded by Grud's disappearance, she thrust the mirror in front of his face and wished him far away too. He vanished. Tara hoped they were indeed both far away now, but as she went to put Scathantar into its pouch, it suddenly faded from her hand.

Panicking, Tara searched around her. Mawgan put his hand on her arm and said, 'It has served its purpose. Its use is three times.' Tara nodded, she had forgotten.

They hurried on to the passageway.

'We must get to Craebh Ciuil, my mother's wand.' Donella told them. 'It is said that when the heir to the kingdom is in need, the case where it is kept will open and the heir can take it. We need it to fight Marvaanagh, she is much worse than you could possibly know. Her magical abilities are great.'

'We have discovered that. Where is this wand kept,' asked Mawgan.

'In the chambers that once belonged to my parents. But we must hurry, time is short.'

Time was always short in the Otherworld, thought Tara.

'Have you seen a little girl anywhere?' asked Jared.

'As I said, I have not seen any human children.'

'I don't mean Tara's sister, I mean Leanne. She's a little realm girl, and invisible.'

Donella stared at Jared as if he was a little simple. How annoying, thought Tara, more so because it reminded her of her own behaviour towards Jared.

Tara put her arm around him protectively. Clearly, he was upset over Leanne, and it was all her fault for not thinking before she opened her big mouth. 'Someone bewitched Jared. Sylvia the dryad more than likely, and probably Queen Marvaanagh put her up to it. Leanne is invisible, only Jared can see her.'

Donella nodded, her face instantly softening in sympathy. She turned, and closed the passage door leaving them in darkness once more.

They found it surprisingly easy to reach the chamber after the initial stumbling around in the secret passageway. They must have caught Queen Marvaanagh by surprise, but by now she must realise they had foiled the Dullahan.

Something was niggling at Tara as they walked. She had the strongest feeling she was close to solving the mystery, that the answer lay there somewhere right before her eyes. If she could just put her finger on it...but it would have to wait, they had other things they must do.

Donella led the way into the chamber, being careful to close the door behind them. She went to a portrait on the wall and lifted it down. They all crowded around to look into the glass case embedded in the wall. Lying inside was what must be the wand. It didn't look like much, just a small, silver, tree branch. But if it could fight the magic of Marvaanagh it must be powerful, Tara thought.

There seemed to be no way of opening the case. 'Only the true heir of the realm can take it,' said Tara quickly, remembering what Princess Gwyn had told them. She didn't know why, but she had a sudden thought Donella must not touch it.

Donella saw her expression and declared stubbornly, 'I am the true heir and now I need the case to open.'

'Yes, we need the case to open,' repeated Niamh.

Tara's niggle became stronger and all of a sudden it was like the little pieces of a jigsaw puzzle coming together. It couldn't have happened if she hadn't seen Donella and witnessed her stubborn ways, but now she knew.

At the same moment, the case opened. With a cry of happiness, Donella reached in to take the wand. Tara grabbed her wrist and pulled it away shouting, 'Niamh must take the wand! Only Niamh! You mustn't touch it, Donella!'

Everyone stared at her transfixed by her outburst. Tara quickly took the opportunity to guide Niamh's hand towards Craebh Ciuil. Mawgan tried to intervene.

'Don't!' said Tara. 'I know what I'm doing, I know everything now. You have to trust me!'

Niamh felt around. The wand glowed for a second, and as if magnetised, moved towards her hand.

'It feels right,' Niamh declared, as she removed the wand.

'I do not understand,' said Donella. 'I am the heir. I wear the heir's bracelet.'

Tara smiled a knowing smile. 'No, Niamh is the heir and she wears the bracelet.'

They all turned as the chamber door suddenly crashed open, banging against the wall, a woman stood there, her beautiful face filled with fury. She wore a long, multicoloured, satin dress, her hair, again just like Niamh's and Donella's, curly and black, reached to her waist. Queen Marvaanagh!

'That wand is mine, give it to me,' she demanded.

Grislic goblins filled the room. They grabbed Jared and Mawgan and pulled them out into the hallway. A goblin snatched Swifan, and Tara heard a cry of frustration as it dissolved in his hand.

Lucy and Donella dashed across the room to join Niamh and Tara hard up against the wall. Niamh held up the wand in front them in the hope of warding off both magic and goblins.

'Free us, or be sorry,' demanded Mawgan. 'My uncle will be here soon.' He tried to hit out, but with four goblins on each arm, struggled in vain.

Somewhere behind him, stood Zalen. Jared was right – a traitor. Zalen caught Tara's eye, then disappeared from view.

Marvaanagh mumbled some words under her breath and raised her hand. A horrendous roar caused Tara to stiffen, and she ducked back as a gust of wind come spiralling towards them.

Tara held tight to Niamh's arm, her intention to help her with her wand. Craebh Ciuil had other ideas and dragged Niamh's hand upwards, sparks burst from it, scattering down over them.

The wind reversed, knocking over some of the grislic goblins. Marvaanagh fell back and hit the wall before dropping to the floor. The goblins closest to her, blew out through the door.

Marvaanagh recovered quickly, promptly leaping to her feet. She turned to Tara. 'I knew you would be trouble. Hard to kill, but not impossible.' With that, she flung out her arm and the room lit up as a bolt of lightning arched towards them. Again Craebh Ciuil moved by itself, shielding Tara.

The lightning bolt hit Niamh's bracelet, and they fell together against the wall to the side of a big window knocking over Donella and Lucy, it rebounded back towards Marvaanagh who ducked out of the way.

Electricity rippled through Tara's body, causing a mild shock. It was enough to startle her momentarily and she struggled to grasp Niamh's arm, to prevent her from dropping the wand.

Shaken, but determined, Niamh kept a good grip. How awful it must be not to be able to see what was going on, thought Tara. How brave and noble of her.

'What do we do now?' Tara said, as Marvaanagh glared at her, pure evil in her eyes. Immediately, Tara knew it wasn't just protection they needed, but to fight Marvaanagh's magic. But Niamh didn't know any magic. All she had was the wand and her abilities to move things or hold them back. Surely the wand would enhance any magic Niamh had.

Tara searched for something to move. A large portrait hung on the wall above Marvaanagh's head. Quickly Tara whispered to Niamh and taking her arm, she aimed Craebh Ciuil at it. Niamh screwed up her sightless eyes in concentration. As Marvaanagh stretched her hand out towards them once more, the portrait fell and hit her on the shoulder.

Marvaanagh crumpled, but managed to stay on her feet, her

expression murderous. She raised her hand at the ceiling. The elaborately carved wood began to split and crack. It rained down in huge chunks. Before it reached them, Craebh Ciuil, sparks flying, began turning it to dust.

Marvaanagh took the opportunity to fire off a volley of hail at them. Craebh Ciuil counteracted, sending it back. It missed Marvaanagh and bounded off the walls and ceiling, showering down on the remaining goblins. Shielding their heads, they ran out into the hall.

Niamh had lost all control, too tired to keep up with it all. Her arm dropped. Tara spurred her on, and with one last effort, Niamh raised the wand and sent portraits flying off the walls towards Marvaanagh. They tumbled down on her, but she held out her hand, deflecting them all.

Marvaanagh let out a sneering laugh; she pointed her hand downwards shouting strange words. The door slammed, shutting out the goblins, Jared and Mawgan, leaving Tara, Niamh, Donella and Lucy with Marvaanagh.

Marvaanagh stepped onto the painting that had hit her shoulder. It began to rise in the air. At the same time, the floor began to shake. Tara could hardly believe her eyes when water began to bubble through the floorboards. More water burst through the floor in several other places. It rapidly rose to their knees.

Donella waded to the window, but couldn't open it. 'I cannot swim,' she cried.

Lucy began to whimper.

'It's okay,' said Tara. 'Donella, come here to Lucy, on this side of me.' She pointed to her left. 'I'm sure you'll be okay in the water. Trust me on this.'

Tara grabbed Niamh; she would need help with Craebh Ciuil.

Marvaanagh rose up higher on her floating picture, laughing. 'Drown you troublesome children!'

Tara felt the familiar tingling in her legs and her fingers were webbing. She held up her hand to show Donella.

Donella lifted her hand and sure enough, her fingers had begun to web too. Tara leant over and whispered encouragement, saying she would explain later.

Donella grabbed Lucy now with both hands as Tara spotted a swish of a tail beneath the water. Donella's eyes grew wide with shock. Tara's own tail was fully-grown too and she held Niamh with ease.

Niamh, with both hands free, began to swirl then twist the wand. She twisted it around and around.

'What are you doing, Niamh?' Tara hissed, as she struggled to keep both her own Niamh's head above water.

'I'm not sure. Craebh Ciuil is talking to me, telling me what to do.'

As Niamh twirled the wand, the water began to spin. Faster and faster it swirled into a whirlpool, dragging in more and more water until it began to form a funnel. It caught them all up and soon Tara and Niamh rose in the air, Donella and Lucy dragged in with them.

'Jaredddddd!' shouted Lucy in panic.

Marvaanagh was trying to avoid the funnel by using the picture as a flying carpet, dodging it this way and that, but the funnel followed her until at last it caught her in the top. Suddenly the bottom part of the funnel broke way, the water splashing back onto the floor taking Tara, Niamh, Lucy and Donella with it. They landed safely in the remaining pool as the water began to drain back through the floorboards.

Marvaanagh stood on top of the twisting whirlpool as it came down sideways, crashing her and the picture through the window. Tara swam to the window just in time to see Marvaanagh landing with a great splash in the fountain. The rest of the water subsided leaving them all sitting on the floor. Tara and Donella's tails swishing around like floundered fish.

A commotion in the hall alerted them – more people! Tara

waited in trepidation for the worst to happen, but in through the door burst King Branwalather with his troops, followed by Jared and Mawgan. The king exclaimed aloud when he saw the two mermaids. Mawgan raised his eyebrows on seeing Donella, who shrugged.

Within a few moments, Tara and Donella's tails turned back to legs. Tara struggled to her feet and looked out of the window to see what was happening with Marvaanagh.

The inner ward had filled with troops and she watched as Marvaanagh dragged herself out of the fountain. Spotting her at the window, Marvaanagh fired a look of pure evil at Tara – her eyes taking on a staring sinister look. They began to glow yellow, a familiar, mustard yellow.

Before anyone could do anything, Marvaanagh jumped up, and coiling around in a spiral of mist, transformed into a large brown hare. She dodged between the legs of the soldiers and through into the outer ward. Several of the soldiers took off after her.

Chapter Twenty-Two

Mawgan had dispatched soldiers to search the castle for Niamh's scarf. Everyone else had warm drinks, and a fire roared away in the two fireplaces at each end of the great hall. Tara and Donella had changed into dry clothes. Being much of the same height, Tara was able to borrow a dress and shoes.

'I think you have some explaining to do, Tara,' said King Branwalather, he took off his gauntlet and rested his hand on the great mantelpiece above the fire. 'We would all like to know how you worked the mystery out.'

Tara had everyone's attention – Donella and Niamh especially.

'Well, I kept thinking about the time,' Tara began. 'Time seems to pass quicker here. That kept niggling at me. Then when I saw Donella, she reminded me of someone. At first, I thought it was Niamh, but when Donella looked at Jared in a certain way...well, I almost had it. It came to me just in time before Donella took the wand. Time does go quicker here. Donella reminds me of me because she's my sister, I just know she is.'

'But I also wear the bracelet of the heir,' said Donella. 'Though I now believe I am not the heir.'

Tara didn't know how to explain this. Niamh was sitting in an armchair and Tara went over and held up her arm. 'Niamh wears the real bracelet and it does protect her – she survived the Dullahan.'

Donella showed her own bracelet. 'I do not know if this is real or not.'

'Let me see it, my dear,' Branwalather asked Donella, indicating for her to take it off.

'I cannot remove it,' said Donella. 'I never could.'

'You should be able to, just like me,' said Niamh. 'Let me try the wand.'

Donella helped her guide Craebh Ciuil to it. As soon as the wand touched the bracelet, the stone in it transformed to a clear glass. Suddenly, Donella's hair changed from black and curly, to strawberry-blonde and straight, her eyes as green as the sea. They all gasped. Now Donella looked very like Tara.

'The bracelet must have been bewitching Donella!' said Mawgan, amazed. 'That is why she could not remove it. Yes, time does move quicker in the realms, though it does not seem so to us, about half as fast again than in the human world, so ten human years is fifteen here. I had quite forgotten.'

Donella ran to a huge mirror hanging on the wall and stood there staring at her reflection. She moved her head this way and that and turning to look at Tara, she suddenly smiled. 'I look so much better. I always hated the way I looked, it was never right. I also have a sister...' She paused. '...and a family, somewhere in the human world. Oh my goodness!' Her smile faded and she turned and looked at Niamh. 'I am most sorry for you. Your parents are trapped on Ynys Is.'

A thoughtful expression crossed Niamh's features, but she didn't speak.

'You still have family, Niamh,' said King Branwalather, his eyes warming. '*I* am your uncle. You also have Princess Gwyn who is your aunt. And you still have your human family...though I am unsure of just how human they are...' He reached over and patted Niamh's hand.

'Thank you, U-Uncle,' said Niamh tentatively.

Tara, put her arm around her.

'I knew something was amiss,' explained King Branwalather. I was suspicious about the message that was sent to me, and not by my usual messenger. Of course, it had not escaped my notice that Niamh had a close family resemblance. Something was not right, of that I was certain. I sent the captain of my guard back to Dumnonia with a troop of men. At this point, an elf from the village came upon us with a message to go to Caer Searesby. We immediately turned back with my personal guard to follow Mawgan. After all, he is my one and only heir.'

Mawgan looked with affection at his uncle and smiled.

'I became more concerned,' King Branwalather continued, 'when we found Mawgan's horse. On reaching Caer Searesby, the goblins were no match for my soldiers.'

'No, indeed, Uncle,' said Mawgan seriously, 'compared to fighting the Kawpangians.'

King Branwalather raised one eyebrow and nodded. 'Now I want to hear the whole story from the beginning, Tara.'

Tara was curious about who gave the elf the message to come and help, but as the king's face set into a serious expression, she dutifully told her story. She began with the story Uncle Fergus told them, and how they found the photograph album. When she reached the part where she and Jared were first on the forest path following the stag and it had indicated Niamh's scarf in the bracken, Donella interrupted her. 'A white stag?' she asked.

'Yes, it was a white stag.'

'Oh, thank goodness,' said Donella. 'He is *my* stag, I am sure. He has been with me as long as I can remember. My aunt had locked him in a pen. I always went and spent time with him. One day I managed to open the gate and free him. I am so happy he is safe.'

That made sense to Tara, and must be why the stag and helped them. What a wonderful beast.

Suddenly, they heard a commotion outside the hall. Two soldiers entered dragging Zalen. He was shouting. 'I have the scarf! Princess Niamh's scarf!'

'Let him be,' shouted Mawgan. 'He has assisted us in many ways.'

Zalen came towards Niamh's chair and tied the scarf loosely around her neck. 'It was protected by a glamour spell, so that is why no one had yet found it.'

Niamh rubbed her eyes. She looked around at everyone. 'I...I can see – see you all.' She paused, getting used to being able to see again. Her eyes came to rest on Donella. 'Gosh, Donella, I thought I was looking at Tara then. You look the same!'

Tara gave her a kiss on her cheek. 'I'm so happy you can see again. I thought you might be blind forever and it would be all my fault.'

'I sent Zalen after my uncle to bring some troops to help us,' Mawgan explained. 'In case he arrived here ahead of us and Marvaanagh caught him, I did not tell you of this. Zalen I am sure would have cooked up some believable story to cover himself and I would not want you to give him away, but to show you thought him a traitor.'

'I did not want to leave you,' said Zalen. 'It was my fault all this happened. I ran to the village and sent a messenger, an old friend, to intercept King Branwalather. Meantime, I hurried on to Caer Searesby, and avoiding Queen Marvaanagh, persuaded the grislic goblins you had held me prisoner and I had managed to escape your clutches. I also told the goblins you would not come until later in the day, as one of you had been injured by the worm. But unfortunately they spotted you crossing the moat.'

'How was it your fault all this happened, Zalen?' questioned the king.

'I am the one who changed the babies. I knew who Niamh was all along. At first, I was afraid of Queen Marvaanagh and what she would do, and often thought of abandoning you all. But after talking to Princess Gwyn, I began to see I needed to make amends.'

Tara could hardly take this all in. So, she had been right in thinking they should be wary of Zalen, but also right he had tried to help them, even though he was afraid.

'So why didn't you tell us who Niamh was?'

'Princess Gwyn, asked me not to. I would not be believed and there was only one way to prove Niamh was the real heir – she must take Craebh Ciuil.'

'I see,' King Branwalather said, and scratched his chin. 'That is certainly true. To reach Craebh Ciuil, meant coming to Caer Searesby and confronting my sister, Marvaanagh.'

'I hope you believe me when I say that I am most heartily sorry for what I did,' Zalen pleaded. 'Perhaps one day you will forgive me. I do not expect that now, but in time.'

Tara didn't know whether to be angry or comforted at all the information. She decided it might be best not to say anything for now and think about what it meant later. It was a terrible thing Zalen had done. 'There's only one thing left now,' she said. 'We just need to find my – I mean our – father.'

'I may be able to help with that,' said Zalen. He smiled lopsidedly, which wasn't very pleasant, making Tara thankful he didn't smile that much. He turned and hobbled out of the door. When he came back, a man accompanied him. A tall man with auburn hair and lime green eyes. He wore clothing similar to that of the fae folk – a baggy white shirt and grey trousers, his feet were bare.

Tara was astounded. Could it be? 'That's my dad!' she cried. 'I know him from the photos!' She ran over and flung her arms around him. Everything would be all right now, she thought. Mum would be all right, she just knew it. She would have both her parents back.

Her dad stood looking bewildered. 'Tara...my Tara...all grown up!' He looked around. 'And my baby...Niamh, where is she?'

'That's you,' said Niamh to Donella.

Donella didn't move. Tara ran over and grabbed her hand. 'He's your dad too!' Donella shyly went over and Tara pulled her in for a hug. It was difficult for all of them.

Tara glanced towards Niamh whose sad expression touched her heart. Tara went to her. 'You'll always be my sister, Niamh.'

Niamh smiled. 'Yes, we're sisters, always will be.'

Tara's dad sat down with them, and once more she explained the story. Sadness came into his eyes as he listened. He had missed her growing up. A feeling of sadness overcame her too and she choked on her words.

Taking her hand, her dad kissed it. 'It could be worse you know, darling,' he said. 'I might still be a stag roaming the forest, and missed even more years. At least I saw Donella growing up. Your poor mother missed it though.'

'Why didn't Marvaanagh kill you,' Tara asked. 'Why change you into a stag?' Seeing her dad's puzzled face, she realised he didn't know.

'It was the easiest thing at the time,' said Zalen. 'My mistress – erm, I mean the queen, did not have time to clear away corpses.'

Tara shivered.

'The nature of the enchantment,' continued Zalen, 'meant the queen could not kill your father unless she lifted it first, but that would lift all the enchantments.'

'I see,' said Tara's dad. 'The memories are fast coming back to me. Passed down in our family was a story about there being a gateway in the mound. I thought it was an old wives' tale, until I passed through it that night. I don't remember much else, until I found myself transformed into a stag and confined in a pen. It took me a while to realise Donella, as everyone called her, was really Niamh. For all the change of hair and eye colour, I knew my own daughter.'

'How did you change back,' asked Lucy.

'I think I know,' said Zalen. 'Something happened in here. I had just found the scarf, when through one of the upper windows I saw a flash coming from the great hall. At the same time, the stag I saw standing down in the castle grounds changed back into a human. I dashed down to assist him, as he stumbled around, totally naked and bewildered.'

Lucy giggled. Tara's dad blushed.

'That would have been when Niamh touched Donella's

bracelet with the wand,' said Tara. 'When it changed Donella's hair and eyes, it must have changed you back into a human, Dad.'

'You both have so much to tell me...especially you, Tara,' said Dad, sounding a little like Uncle Fergus. 'I've missed your mum too, very much.'

Tara looked from her father to her sister. She laughed to herself. All this time she had imagined having a little sister, instead she had a big sister, how weird. But it was also quite cool really, as she would have someone to watch out for her for a change.

'What happens now though?' Zalen asked. 'Marvaanagh escaped. I could never understand how she travelled the leys so frequently. I thought it was a huge magical secret. All the time she simply shape shifted. Animals can safely travel the leys. They are not at risk. So simple, yet I could never work it out. It is not easy to shape shift, I can tell you by experience, and harder for the queen as it is not so natural for her. So once a hare it would be difficult for her to change back easily. How she managed to conjure up the Gogges Worm and the Dullahan, I do not know. But it would not have been spontaneous, it would have taken much planning. We just have to hope she does not have access to more powerful magic, than we can imagine.'

'I think at some point we are still to find that out, Zalen,' said King Branwalather, the ice back in his eyes, causing him to look fierce. 'We do not know to where my sister has fled, although I suspect back to Glastenning. We will search for her – you can be sure of that. She has committed crimes against these realms. I now also suspect she had a hand in betraying the secrets of Dumnonia to the Kawpangians. It is no wonder we have so many attacks.'

'Queen Marvaanagh also has the map to Ynys Is,' said Zalen forlornly. 'It needs to be returned to my people. I am the one who stole it. Perhaps the queen used it to trap Queen Anya and King

Edmwnd...'

What a mess, thought Tara. But at least they had succeeded in what they came here to do, find her sister and father, and discover who Niamh really was.

While eating a scrumptious feast, prepared by King Branwalather's servants, Tara and Donella chatted to each other, both a little shy at first, but soon it was as if they had always known each other. They both wondered about their own shape shifting abilities.

'We are connected to the realms somehow,' mused Tara. 'And I think it has something to do with Uncle Fergus.'

'I never learnt to swim,' said Donella. 'I was too much watched and confined. Do you think Marvaanagh knows about us?'

'I don't think so, we were under the water and I don't think she saw us.'

Donella frowned. 'I have a feeling it will take time to discover what it all means. But for now I must go and speak with Mawgan.'

Donella walked over to Mawgan and took his hand; they went to discuss everything in private. Tara knew this must affect their betrothal. Donella, no longer the heir, was a human – though of course part mermaid – perhaps merrow.

Tara went over to speak with Jared who leant on the sill staring out of the window onto the inner ward. 'I'm sorry about Leanne,' she said. 'I shouldn't have shouted to shut the door.'

'W-what? Oh that. Well, you weren't to know. You couldn't see her. She was real to me. Do you think she was real, or just a bewitchment? I feel strange now that she's gone.'

'I don't know,' said Tara. 'If she was imaginary, let's hope the spell was lifted and she just disappeared – or if real – escaped somewhere. I'm sorry all the same, more sorry than you'll ever know.' When Jared had cried over Leanne, Tara had seen the inside of him, his soft centre underneath all the bravado. She kissed his cheek. Jared smiled and pulled her hair.

Mawgan and Donella came back and went off to speak privately to King Branwalather. When they came back, they explained how the betrothal papers would be invalidated. Mawgan and Donella would need time to think about things. They were young and had much time to make such major decisions for themselves. Everything had changed. Donella would visit her own world – spend time with her parents as well as Tara. After hearing about Uncle Fergus, she was looking forward to meeting him too.

They all went into the outer ward to get some fresh air. Tara walked with Donella.

'Wait until you meet Uncle Fergus,' said Tara. 'He's great fun. Mum's a bit distant though sometimes. She gets what Uncle Fergus calls *distracted*. It's because of what happened. She doesn't remember on the outside, but deep down she must.'

'I cannot wait to meet them,' said Donella. 'I never had a real family before, only my beloved stag. My aunt...erm, Niamh's aunt, showed me no affection. I spent much of my time playing with all the animals, the castle cats and kittens, and Stag of course.'

Niamh, Jared, Lucy and Zalen who had been lagging behind joined them.

'I hate to leave you behind, Niamh,' said Tara sadly.

'I need to stay here and get to know everyone,' said Niamh. 'I want to see my Aunt Gwyn and spend time with her, find out more about my parents and how they became trapped. Perhaps if the map is found, they can be freed.'

'Gosh Niamh, I keep forgetting, you're a princess now. I'll miss you so much.'

'Now you have returned to your own land, Niamh,' said Zalen. 'You can safely go back to the human world, though it would be difficult at first, so best to stay for awhile, until it is known for sure any residue of the curse put on you has dissipated. What a stroke of luck you did not stay past your eleventh birthday.'

Tara wondered if it was just luck, or whether Uncle Fergus knew more than she suspected and had secretly encouraged them. There were too many coincidences.

Tara took Niamh's hand. 'I'll miss you very much, Niamh.'

'I'll miss you the most,' Lucy insisted. 'You're my best friend.'

They talked about how they would explain it all to Lucy and Jared's parents and Uncle Fergus and Mum. But decided they would figure it out when they got home. They would all travel back to Vrogoly Palace on horseback, leaving Niamh there. After what was sure to be painful goodbyes, they would then travel on to Caer Sidi, and pass through the gateway in the normal way, rather than by ley. From Caer Sidi, which they knew of as Stonehenge, they would phone Uncle Fergus and ask him to pick them up.

* * *

Uncle Fergus hadn't said much when he arrived to collect them, it was as if they had just gone out to Stonehenge for the day, and their uncle had come to pick them up. He just made jokes as usual and shook hands with Tara's dad, his younger brother, whom he hadn't seen for ten years. But they looked at each other, smiled and nodded.

They dropped off Jared and Lucy at their own house, where their parents greeted them in a normal way. How strange no one had missed them, thought Tara, hoping it would be the same for her.

On reaching the house, hesitatingly, Tara opened the back door. Mum was putting something into the fridge. Uncle Fergus tapped her on the shoulder and she turned.

'Ahh, there you are, dear, we've missed you so much while

you were at boarding school. Look we've prepared a feast for you. Now come and have a hug.' She opened her arms out wide.

Donella ran into them and they shared their first hug for ten years.

Tara looked at the kitchen table – instead of the usual mountains of food – there was a simple pan of stew and an apple crumble. She smiled and joined in the hug.

Epilogue

The huge raven flew over the mound and crossed into the garden, landing on the kitchen window ledge. Tara was watching. She shivered. She recognised it as the one she saw at the mound last year, then later at Caer Sidi when she and Jared met the Mordanta, and again when it had attacked the Gogges Worm.

It was almost a year to the day since they had passed through the gateway into the Realm of Wiltunscire – a year almost to the day when she had last seen the raven.

What was it? Who was it? What did it want? Tara had the feeling she would find out very soon...

OUR STREET
BOOKS

Our Street Books for children of all ages, deliver a potent mix of fantastic, rip-roaring adventure and fantasy stories to excite the imagination; spiritual fiction to help the mind and the heart grow; humorous stories to make the funny bone grow; historical tales to evolve interest; and all manner of subjects that stretch imagination, grab attention, inform, inspire and keep the pages turning. Our subjects include Non-fiction and Fiction, Fantasy and Science Fiction, Religious, Spiritual, Historical, Adventure, Social Issues, Humour, Folk Tales and more.